Enoch Fitch Burr

**The Stars of God**

Enoch Fitch Burr

**The Stars of God**

ISBN/EAN: 9783337038373

Printed in Europe, USA, Canada, Australia, Japan

Cover: Foto ©Andreas Hilbeck / pixelio.de

More available books at **www.hansebooks.com**

# THE STARS OF GOD.

BY

E. FITCH BURR, D. D., LL. D.

AUTHOR OF
ECCE CŒLUM, PATER MUNDI, AD FIDEM, ETC.

---

" WHEN I CONSIDER THY HEAVENS."

HARTFORD. :
THE STUDENT PUBLISHING COMPANY,
1896.

# CONTENTS.

# I.

# THE EARTH.

## I.

# THE EARTH.

The earth is naturally the first round of the ladder by which our knowledge climbs toward the astronomical summits of the universe.

So let us begin at home—as our charities and duties and travels are compelled to do—that is, at the star that lies nearest to us, the star that is so near that it cannot be nearer, the star on which we live.

For the earth is a star. This assertion would have astonished the ancients. And to not a few in our own times it is "a hard saying—who can hear it? What! this great, dull outspread of plains and mountains and waters like the bright points that spangle the evening vault! It cannot be. Our senses protest." And yet if we could be freed from the chains of gravity and go away indefinitely from the earth we should find its surface gradually contracting and levelling and brightening on our sight until at last it, too, would appear as a bright point on the sky surrounded on all sides by vacancy—in all respects one of the great sisterhood of stars that make the glory of our nights.

Our earth is not only a star, but is by far the most interesting and important to us of all the stars.   This is saying too much to suit some, and too little to suit others.   For our earth has extravagant admirers—also extravagant revilers.   Some can hardly say too much for it, and some can hardly say too much against it.   Some are disposed to worship it, and some to crucify it.   Some have no other deity than earthly things and serve them devotedly all their lives, though without the formality of altar and prayers ; while to others the world is a mud-monster, defiled and defiling— a sort of reptilian devil to be loathed and fought to the utmost.   These extremes must settle their quarrel between themselves.   We can side with neither.   We cannot stand with the idolaters ; nor can we stand with the hermits of the Thebaid to whom the world was the sum of all villainies and dangers.   But we can go so far as to say that no other star, in the whole broad heaven, has anything like the interest and value to us which our own star possesses.

It is our cradle, our workshop, and our grave. Of its substance our bodies are made.   From its maternal bosom we get our living, and indeed all the materials of our comfort and civilization. On it we pass our entire probation as moral beings. And on it took place the incarnation, the atonement, and the manifold miracles recorded in our Scriptures—events great enough to consecrate and glorify any world. It furnishes our astronomical instruments, the place on which to plant them, the observers to use them, the mathematics and elementary knowledge of matter to empower them. It supplies the primary school which teaches us all we know about the nature and laws of matter—showing us that it consists of many kinds and that all its kinds, under all circumstances, are subject to one law of mutual attraction which can be used with enormous effect in explaining the distant heavens. The earth really supplies the alphabet from which we construct our astronomy : not only supplies the elementary astronomical letters, but largely puts them together into syllables and words and intelligible sentences.

Just as it is more important for a man to know well his own country than it is to know well a foreign country, so it is more important for us to be well acquainted with our own star than it is to be well acquainted with any other star in all the radiant heavens.

What do we know about this, to us, the most interesting and important of all the stars? Very
much indeed. Almost infinitely more than we
know of any other star. Once it was not so. Not
so very far back, the earth to human ken was
almost a sealed book—let us venture to say a book
sealed with seven seals, though written within and
on the backside. But that time is well past. Men
became inquisitive. Since the earth was nearest
to. them of all the stars; since indeed it was that
on which they dwelt, on which they could move
about freely, and on which they could bring all
their senses to bear in closest observation—what a
fine field for successful inquisitiveness ! So they
began to use to some purpose the most wonderful
instruments of investigation known among men,
viz., their own eyes, ears, hands, feet, brains ;
gradually supplementing these with hammers and
spades and crucibles and batteries and laboratories
and calculuses and optical instruments and steam-
ships and railways. Many ran to and fro and
knowledge was increased. Satan is not the only
observer whose business it is to go to and fro in
the earth, and walk up and down in it. The world
has been ransacked. Floods of travel and investigation have swept over nearly all lands. We have
gone down into valleys, we have scaled mountains,

we have crossed oceans ; the general features of the world are thoroughly understood, and details to an enormous amount. Whole libraries are needed to express them. They could not be told in years though we had 'a brazen throat and a hundred iron tongues.' They have been digested into so many sciences that not single mind can master them all. As much cannot be said of our knowledge of the distant heavens. One may know it all and still be no prodigy. We shall never know another star as well as we do our own —until . . . . . !

Not that our knowledge of the earth is anything like exhaustive. There is reason to suspect that what is known of our star is only a small part of what there is to be known. We have only begun to know the world. As yet we have scarcely done more than skim the surface of things. Our inquiries, like far-flying birds, have only alighted here and there on wide stretches of country. Africa, the two Arctics, and the ocean-depths contain many a secret. So does the most familiar land the sun shines on ; and indeed the most familiar single object about us. No slightest thing within our reach can be considered as perfectly understood. Scores of questions can be asked to which no answers are given or promised.

The Sphinx has many a riddle to read us out of her earth-book which we cannot solve though we die for it.

And, not only is our knowledge of the earth incomplete but we are very far from having gone the length of our tether. Who imagines that we know about the earth all we can know, or are likely to know? Who imagines that we have almost sighted the shore of our ocean—as we see it to day? Our ignorance has the glow of morning on its face. Nature's promises are almost as plentiful as its problems. Mysteries are ever unfolding about us, like the buds of advancing spring. Every science relating to the earth is under marching orders; and the orders are not to retreat but to advance. "Forward. March!— there is yet much land to be possessed"—is in the mouths of all the captains and inscribed on all the banners. And hardly a year passes without advancing the outposts. New sciences are starting up while others are starting forward. Among them all, daily discoveries are the order of the day. All over the world the Pillars of Hercules, the Land's End, and Ultima Thule are being put to flight. Cloistered places are becoming public parks. It seems as if in the matter of knowledge of the earth the little fingers of the future will be

thicker than the loins of the present.    It is better
to be in a slough of Despond than to have a slough
of Despond in us.    Neither of these unpleasant
conditions belongs to the present generation of
scientists.    We are all full of cheerful expectation.

Of course there is an element of uncertainty in
such an outlook on our future.    Divine predictions
always come true : human  predictions often  fail
though made by Magi.    We have occasion to remember that there is many a slip between the cup
and the lip ; that knowledge, like other  things,
has  a way  of ebbing  as well  as flowing ; that
sciences as well as scientists, have been known to
backslide.    But the past is sure.    The knowledge
we *have* gained about the earth we can count upon.
So, we will turn from pleasant dreams of what
will be to sober consideration of the facts already
in hand.

For  much knowledge of our own star we are indebted to the same instruments that have given us
most of onr knowledge  of the distant heavens,
viz., our optical instruments and our mathematics
—the right  and left  hands  of  our astronomy.
Working together these  have  given  us  all  our
accurate geography.  We have  now  determined
with great exactness the latitudes and longitudes
of all the more important points of the earth : we

have also, by the same means and by soundings gained a clear idea of the great ocean beds. Every civilized nation has provided charts of its own coasts so accurately made that they represent the outline of the land and the neighboring sea-bottom with almost the fidelity of a Dutch portrait or of a photograph. This has been done in connection with a system of triangulation in which the telescope and its adjuncts play a conspicuous part. The coaster and fisherman as they feel their way safely among the shoals and sunken rocks may thank for their safety, not their stars indeed, but the same instrument that has done the most at exploring the stars.

The telescope is also the condition of all extensive ocean-voyaging. The coast surveys provide for the convenience and safety of navigation along certain shores; but if we are to have that knowledge of the wide earth that comes from immense commerce and travel, means must be furnished for passing over the trackless oceans freely and safely in every direction. In order to do this, the sailor must be able to find his exact place on the deep at any moment. And it is not enough for him to consult his dead reckoning and chronometer; he must verify these by observing certain heavenly bodies and by consulting the famous Nautical Almanac, which is, in some sort, the sailor's Bible, doing for him on the natural deep what the Bible offers to do on the spiritual deeps. The foundations of the Nautical Almanac are the Greenwich Observatory, the telescope, and the theory of gravitation. These are what we come to if we dig down to the very bottom of things, and ask how that indispensible companion of every long voyage is made. Astronomy hides behind every page of this *vade mecum* which has made the deep comparatively safe, and gradually covered it with inquisitive traffickers and travelers into all lands, and so been the means of a vast accession to our knowledge of the earth. What crowded maps and bulky geographies are now on the tables of our scholars and even on the desks of the common school ? A thoughtful man sees the shadow of a telescope in the background and between the lines of every one of them. That our little children know more of the world on which they live than did the sages of antiquity is due to the fact that the optic tube, pointed at the sky, has discovered more facts on the earth than it has done in the heavens.

In the case of all other stars there is no diffi-culty in telling all we know about them—the known facts are so few. But what we know about the earth is so prodigiously much that if we would have any space left for telling of other stars we must narrow our view to a few general features like those which come under notice in the case of the other stars—such as shape, and size, and situation, and motions.

We find that the ancients were mistaken in thinking that the earth is a rough plain indefinitely extended, resting on solid supports, in the centre of the universe, without motion itself but revolved about by all the heavens. All this is now denied and defied. We know that the earth is globular in form. We know that it has no elephant and immense tortoise to rest upon but is altogether unsupported amid the vacancies of space—literally "hung on nothing." And we know that instead of being forever at rest it is forever in motion after a most astonishing fashion ; and that, so far from being the great central heart of the creation about which all things are framed and to which all things have respect as the seat of honor and control and destiny, it is almost infinitely otherwise. We are sorry to have to charge such great mistakes on the fathers. But they are not without excuse. It is unreasonable to ask men to see as well at dawn as at noon. The shadows of the night are bound to retire gradually. We ourselves are often misled by first seemings just as the fathers were.

We are largely indebted to the telescope for all our precise and minute knowledge of the shape and size of the earth. Its general roundness is known by other means (men who have sailed or railroaded round the world need no other proof), but we have to use the telescope with its appliances in order to know that we do not live on a proper globe, but on one that is somewhat flattened on opposite sides ; and also to know what are the exact values of the longest and shortest diameter. This knowledge is best gained by measuring arcs of a meridian in various parts of the world ; and telescopes have been indispensable to such measurements. By these it has been found that our extremes of diameter differ by about twenty-six miles while our mean diameter is 7912 miles.

This spheroidal star turns around on its shortest diameter once in twenty-four hours, without the least noise or jar, carrying us with a perfectly uniform motion through space at the rate of a thousand miles an hour, and making the whole heavens seem to revolve about us daily. In addition, the earth wheels about the sun once a year— which means that while we are being carried round the earth at a thousand miles an hour we are also being carried about the sun at more than sixty times that rate. It almost makes one dizzy to think of such complicate and tremendous veloci-ties. Perhaps we feel an instinctive prompting to grasp at something. Perhaps we seem to be losing our breath—if our imaginations are very alert. But we are safe. Mother earth clasps her children mightily to her bosom as she flies. She is careful to carry with us in our double motion the atmos-phere and all our surroundings without disturbing in the least their relative positions ; and to shoot along as softly and silently and smoothly as she does swiftly. Were it not for this we should find our rushing somersaults and gyrations through space anything but comfortable. As it is, not a hint of our break-neck journeying comes directly to our senses. We have to infer it distantly but conclusively from the fact that such journeying furnishes the simplest and a perfect explanation of the daily and yearly changes observed in the sky.

By its double motion our star becomes a grand observatory from which to study the other stars. Our common observatories are fixtures. Once built they stand on the same spot as long as they stand at all. If they were only easily transferable from one point of the earth to anoher—could be cheaply and smoothly spirited away from Greenwich to Cape Town or Quito or, better still, to a point some hundreds of millions of miles nearer the heavenly bodies than we now are, it would sometimes be a great convenience. Well, this is done by means of that underlying observatory that we call the earth. This is the great celestial lookout.

By its rounded form and transparent atmosphere and position among the stars it gives us a grand outlook on the populous heavens. By turning on its axis it brings successively into view all parts of the sky ; whereas without this rotation we could see only a single hemisphere, except by travelling half round the globe. By its movement about the sun it brings us nearly 200 millions of miles nearer some of the stars than we should be without this motion, and so enables us to discover important facts not otherwise obtainable. And then this travelling observatory of ours, ponderous and granite-built as it is, moves so smoothly and quickly from place to place that no senses nor instruments, however delicate, can detect the slightest disturbance. It is so stoutly built of endless "munitions of rocks" that we have done our best at describing firmness and stability in a thing when we have likened it to the foundations of the earth and the everlasting hills. Admirable Uraniberg !—ready made to hand, vast in size, sumptuous in appointments beyond any palace we ever saw, usable by everybody without charge and with equal freedom (knock at the door of any other first class observatory for a like privilege and see what you will get,) built and kept in repair without a penny of cost to any man, carrying us and all our secondary observatories with magnificent swiftness and comfort on great journeys of discovery and astonishment among the constellations—surely this is a wonderful OBSERVATORY, well deserving to be written in capitals !

# II.

# THE MOON.

## II.

# THE MOON.

We are outward-bound. And the first star we come to is the one to which we should next give our attention.

The old Greek poet Æschylus pictures to us Agamemnon, king of men, reclining night after night on the roof of the Atridæ at Mycenæ, and, propped on his elbow, watching the round silver shield of Dian as it beamed upon him from above. Still earlier, Homer gives us this picture of a moon-lit scene on the battle fields of Troy, where lie with upturned faces the sleeping heroes of yesterday and to-morrow : "As when in heaven the stars around the glittering moon beam loveliest amid the breathless air, and in clear outline appear every hill, sharp peak, and woody dell— deep upon deep the sky breaks open, and each star shines forth, while joys fills the shepherd's heart." Let us give a more modern picture.

It is night. You are abroad among the shadows —as perhaps you ought not to be. What are commonly called the stars are shining ; but their light is too small to make plain an unfamiliar road. You stumble, you slip into a slough, you take the wrong turn, you run against some person as be-nighted as yourself; in short you wish that you had taken a lantern. And, lo, what you wish is furnished you—a lantern with the lighting of which neither you nor I had anything to do.

What is that? In your hesitating and perplexed progress your eye happens to rest on the east. A narrow streak of nebulous whiteness lies along the horizon. It slowly broadens and brightens, and soon a silver rim presents itself which by imperceptible degrees expands into a complete circle, flushed more or less with gold. Now the objects about you begin to show clearly. The dim, stumbling, vexatious road stumbles and vexes no longer. Every moment improves the situation. By the time the moon has mounted above the trees your troubles are at an end. Now you can walk safely and conveniently all night if you will ; for the Heavenly Father has sent his own lantern to your rescue. And a brave lantern it is—its soft, kindly beams doing hundreds of times as much in the way of illumination as all the stars put to-gether. You go on your way rejoicing.

This scene is a sample of what has been all the way back to Adam—and longer. The moon is no stranger. Men have walked in the light of it as long as they have walked at all. It has shone in every sky. Its name appears in every known language. It has looked down on every human generation and been to it for signs and seasons and days and years. Itself substantially unchanged, it has seen the rise and fall of empires and civilizations and dispensations and geologic æons even. No doubt the moon goes back to the world's beginning. And, pray, when was that? Who knows? A plenty of guesses there are : some founded on geological considerations (fogs), some on astronomical considerations (another sort of fogs), and some on no considerations at all (not even fogs) but all the guesses enormously at war with one another. *I* guess that as soon as the earth was swinging on its way the moon was swinging in its sky—and that was millions of years ago.

What an antique? Ye who hunt the neighborhoods through for old furniture, who ransack the by-ways of Europe for originals by the old masters : ye who spade among the graves of nations for relics of primal Greece and Egypt and Assyria and count a *find* rusty with 4000 years as beyond all price—what think you of that celestial antiquity, the old, old moon, that from the beginning or ever the earth was has hung its cheery lantern in the sky ! There is genuine antiquity for you, without the hunting and digging ! And, for aught we can see, the relic is as good as new. The moon carries no marks of its mighty years. It is not faded, worn, tottering, dim-eyed, the worse for wear. We see no reason for thinking it does not shine as brightly and go on its way as vigorously as it ever did : no reason for thinking it cannot go on its round of aspects and motions with unflagging strength, world without end.

A famous traveler ! Has been journeying time out of mind. Not along the lands and seas where as yet our travel is compelled to go, but along the stretches of the sky where our travel is ambitious of going. A fine post for observation has the Queen of night had as she has rolled round the world on her flashing wheel. All that makes history has passed beneath her beaming eye. If she could speak how much she would have to tell. What additions and subtractions she could make to the story of the nations ! How much of what is called history would have to blush for itself and consent to be called fiction !

What is this comely Queen of night, this exalted observer, this famous traveller, this mute but capable historian, this antique but not antiquated celestial, this delightful painter of field and flood and ruins old—of abbeys gray and colosseums grand? It is a *star* just as the earth is. We sometimes speak of the moon *and* stars; but we mean only a distinction as to apparent size. The moon appears larger than what are commonly called stars, merely because it is nearer to us. If we could push it away from us a certain distance it would appear to us as a shining point on the sky.

This moon-star has had the common fate of exalted position—unmeasured praise and also unmeasured abuse. Some have made it out a goddess, and some a devil. Some have worshipped it under the name of Diana, goddess of the silver bow; and some under the name of Hecate, queen of hell and mother of all evils. The worshipping age is past; but the moon has still its great admirers and great abusers. It has more sonnets inscribed to it than the sun itself. Also, the worst stories are told of it; for slander loves a shining mark and is very apt to hit it. All sorts of evil reports have been set on foot against it as being unfriendly to plants and animals. The astrologers of the Middle Ages and later, would have it that moon-beams were poisonous, pest-breeding, especially when coming from the neighborhood of Saturn. There the moon had an evil eye. There it cursed and swore like a pirate. Then let the crops look out for droughts and mildews and blastings. Then let cattle and men look out for debilities, consumptions, convulsions, jaundice, *lunacy.* Wo to him who is born under the "house of the moon"; better not to have been born at all! The bad stories still linger. Dogs are not the only things that bark at the moon. Bad to sleep in the moonlight, is it? Hurts certain grains and timbers, does it? That is slander, not to say superstition. Do not believe a word of it. Smile at it as the Queen herself does. She has a shining faculty for standing abuse; for she shines on good humoredly in a Christian way and never answers back. She knows she would not harm us on any account. That consciousness is enough. And she goes serenely on her way, flinging down her silver on the saucy world as freely as ever. Go thou and do likewise, O much abused reader!

What men knew about the moon till lately was little more than could be learned by the naked eye only. Common observation shows a luminous disc, about half a degree in diameter, variously shaded, apparently moving westward with all the other bright objects in the sky and at the same time creeping eastward among them so as to make a complete circuit in about twenty-seven

days ; in the same period waning from a full disc
to nothing and then waxing back to its old ful-
ness ; in addition suffering occasional eclipses
which after eighteen years repeat themselves in
the same order and at the same intervals as
before.

From this small capital put out at usury, we
have at last come to a large lunar fortune. For
the observed facts just stated are best accounted
for by supposing that the moon is a round earthlike body, situated between the earth and the sun ;
shining by the reflected light of the sun, and
revolving about the earth in twenty-seven days.
This supposition is the simplest possible explanation of the lunar motions and phases and eclipses ;
and in our time the simplest explanation of an
observed fact is the only scientific explanation.
Accordingly we give a scientific answer to the
atheist when we tell him that God is the simplest
explanation of Nature. He ought to be satisfied
with it. No science has any better.

But let us go into particulars as to some of the
chief points of interest in regard to the moon
which have come to us by the combined aid of
observation, a just theory, the mighty mathematics, and the fact that the moon is the nearest to us
of all the heavenly bodies. It is to this nearness

that we owe it that we know far more of the moon than we do of any other object in our sky. In a city it is by no means certain, or even likely, that one knows the most of his nearest neighbor. Perhaps that neighbor is the most unknown person in the whole great community. But, fortunately, in the country it is different. Every man knows every other : and he is apt to know best the man who lives next to him. The moon lives next to us. And the knowledge we have of it is next to that we have of the earth itself.

The shape of the moon is globular. At the full it seems like a somewhat clouded silver plate. Then it looks as if the plate itself was being eaten up, by little and little, by some invisible monster whose supply of eatables had been too scanty. We seem to see on the ragged edge the marks of his teeth. At last all is devoured ; only, however, to reappear in a new crescent and slowly wax to its former roundness. Notwithstanding this apparent variety of shapes—crescent, half circle, gibbous, full circle—the moon has really but one shape, the same the earth has. Only a round body could show the *phases*.

The light of the moon is not its own. If it were self-luminous it would, of course, always appear in full circle. But it is not seen at all when the sun cannot shine on the face that is turned toward us. When the sun is so placed that its beams can touch that face it begins to appear as a thin crescent, and then enlarges as the position of the sun becomes more favorable, until at last we have the full moon. So the glory of the moon is altogether a borrowed one. And it is a great borrower; for it is able to give us from its store a thousand times the light we get from all the heavenly bodies put together, the sun being excepted—to say nothing of what it lavishes on the wastes of space. Happily the lender is so rich that he can afford to lend largely, to lend without interest, and even to lend with the very poorest chance of getting his principal back again.

I have said that the moon is our nearest neighbor. This was known long before the telescope and the modern astronomy, by simply taking the angular distance of the sun from a half-moon. But we know it by better means now. Among all the heavenly bodies none is so much displaced on the sky by a given change of place in the observer as is the moon. This could not be unless the moon were nearer to us than is any other heavenly body. When we have found exactly how much this displacement amounts to we can tell how far from us the moon is. It is about 237000 miles away.

With this distance we can readily find the lunar diameter to be about 2000 miles—a greatness that does not astonish us, but doubtless would have astonished the ancients ; as many of them at least as supposed that the face of the moon was as large as the face of a man.

Not only is the moon our nearest neighbor among the stars, but it is bound to us by still closer ties. The mighty bond of the atttaction of gravitation is upon both of us. We cannot part company if we would. We are held fast by a necessity of nature to an eternal partnership. The moon *must* wheel about the earth and go with it in its annual voyage about the sun, and in whatever other voyages it has occasion to make. Time was when every star was supposed to wheel about the earth and to be helplessly yoked to its fortunes. But we now know that this is true only of the moon. It is our solitary satellite, our one domestic of the old life-long pattern ; or rather it is Ruth saying to Naomi " The Lord do so to me and more also if aught but death part thee and me."

Local neighborhood, especially enforced neigh-borhood, sometimes means war. But in the case of the earth and moon it means peace, good com-panionship, and mutual service. There is not, and never has been, any quarrel between the two stars. They move amicably together through all the months and years. It is true that the moon disturbs our motions somewhat, and we disturb its motions still more ; but what are called disturbances are not struggles to get apart but to get nearer to each other, or, at least, to prevent a wider separation. Their reciprocal action instead of being hostile is altogether friendly. They make the best of the situation. The moon snows us with light, sends healthful tides through our atmosphere and oceans, and though when it wrestles with us by the invisible arms of its attraction it makes our gait somewhat unsteady and indirect as we go our rounds about the sun, it is as a playful child, holding fast by the mother's hand and pulling now this way and now that, somewhat disturbs her movements, but not so as to prevent her going on her way and at last reaching her destination. This figure would be unfortunate if it should be understood to favor the notion of some that the earth is the mother of the moon—the source from which it was derived.

While the moon acts mightily on the earth it receives from its larger companion far more than it gives. It receives thirteen times as much light and more than a hundred times as much attractive force. We are by far the stronger partner in the partnership and able to carry our points with the small stockholder without the least difficulty—just as is usual. What tides we must make in the atmosphere and oceans of the moon if only she has such earthly things! Such things, however, our science has not yet been able to discover. But how can the "man in the moon" get along without air and water? How do you know that there *are* any men in the moon: or, if there are, that they are not so made as not to need air and water? Must all intelligent beings be made after one pattern? What is your notion of omnipotence?

Perhaps some one has said that every man has a side which the public is never permitted to see. At least it ought to be said, for it is true and important. But whether true and important in the case of men or not, it certainly is in the case of the moon. Only one side of the moon is ever shown to us. In going about the earth our satellite carefully keeps the same face turned toward us as does the courtier toward the queen on leaving the presence. This is done by turning round once on its axis during one revolution about us. Instead of making one rotation in twenty-four hours, as the earth does, it proceeds far more liesurely and takes twenty-seven days for the work.

In going about the earth the moon sometimes passes through the earth's shadow, and so is eclipsed. When it comes between us and the sun the latter is eclipsed. These solar and lunar eclipses used to alarm people at large terribly; for they were thought to mean divine displeasure and to forebode all sorts of public calamities. Armies and nations grew pale; and even now a large part of mankind are ill at ease when the sun or moon seems being eaten up by an invisible monster. But they need not be frightened. The only eclipse the public has to fear just now is an eclipse of faith. And they have great occasion to fear that. Indeed, I know of nothing they have so great occasion to fear. Unbelief is a tragedy, a portent, a pit from the bottom of which no star can be seen. Into that pit many are just now falling. They are lunatics—but have not been made such by the moon.

To the naked eye the moon has a diversified face—some parts appearing brighter than others. With a very low telescopic power we see large shaded patches such as appear on maps of the earth to represent the savage and semi-civilized countries. These smooth, dusky patches were at first supposed to be seas, and received names accordingly—as Mare Frigoris, Mare Imbrium, Mare Serenitatis ; which mean the Sea of Cold, the Sea of Showers, the Sea of Serenity. Then why not say so, in plain English ? Did you ever hear of a little thing called *jealousy?* Well, you are to understand that English astronomers did not want to see French or German names fastened on the moon ; and French and German astronomers did not want English names there ; and so all parties compromised on the Latin which were popular with the learned of all countries. These names are still retained though no astronomer now supposes that they stand for water, but for comparatively smooth plains.

Still higher telescopic powers bring out other features. Now our neighbor somehow seems to have managed to fall among thieves in its travels. It looks deplorably in need of some good Samaritan to come along and bind up its wounds ; for, wounded and battered and scarred, as if by the fist of some triumphant bruiser whose mercy is of the smallest and fist of the largest, is the face that to the naked eye seems so brightly cheerful.

A further increase of power turns the scars into ring-shaped figures all over the surface ; and under the best telescopes the rings swell out into

huge craters sometimes greatly below the general
surface and sometimes greatly above ; sometimes
with cones of considerable elevation within, such
as we find in earthly volcanoes, and often with
streaks radiating from them in every direction.
Plainly the moon has been tremendously volcanic
—far beyond anything in the earth's experience.
Such upheavals, such mighty moonquakes, such
belching out of molten rock from the furnaces
within through rifted mountain sides, such ear-
splitting explosions and vociferations into shud-
dering space (supposing air) ! Be thankful that
you were not there to see and hear and suffer.

Many of these crater-mountains are far larger
in proportion to the moon than are our largest
mountains in proportion to the earth. The chief
of them have been named after certain dead
celebrities—as Plato and Copernicus and Kepler
and Tycho. I say *dead* celebrities. Not one of
them could have gotten such honor while living.
But just as soon as he was dead jealousy of him
began to die ; and, by the time he had been dead a
hundred years, men were quite ready to give him
a place in the lunar Westminster Abbey.

Few mountain ranges are found in the moon.
The principal ones are named from earthly ranges
—as the Apennines, the Alps, the Caucasus. The

3

Apennines begin small, rise gradually for 450 miles and then end abruptly in an almost vertical descent of four miles amid a scene of stormy grandeur and wreck without a peer.

Our present instruments bring us within fifty miles of the moon. With the help of photography wonderful maps of the surface have been made that give a better general view of it than we have of the earth. And one far more awe-inspiring. Nowhere else can we get such an idea of what the wreck of Nature and the crush of worlds would be. A mountainous region of the wildest and most savage discription in comparison with which our Switzerlands and Rockies are tame. Enormous chasms and cavities, great mountains overthrown in every direction, mammoth extinct volcanoes, thirty-nine summits higher than Mt. Blanc—to make railroads in such a land would cost more than $20,000 a mile. What an experience in shaking and quaking the moon must have had some day! It is a world turned upside down. It is a carnival of physical disaster. It is petrified wrath. It is as if all the tossings and wrestlings and outbursts of a cosmic Bedlam had been caught at the wildest and stiffened into stone.

This is what Luna seems. But a dreadful seeming does not always cover a dreadful fact. Is it not possible that the extremely rough and shattered state of the moon may help its purpose as a reflector of sunlight to the earth? Is it really the uninhabited desert it has been thought to be— a sort of stellar purgatory—or do lovely vales of Cashmere hide among the lunar Himalayas and furnish delightful homes to beings who, though constituted differently from ourselves in some respects, are yet like us in their power to know and worship the Almighty Builder of worlds?

# III.

# THE SUN.

## III.

# THE SUN.

The sun also is a star—for the same reasons that the earth and moon are stars, and for other reasons besides. It, too, if removed to a certain distance from us would appear as a bright point on the sky.

From the beginning the sun has been the most conspicuous natural object within the range of human vision. Neither on the earth nor in the sky has ever been seen anything so dazzlingly bright, so terribly glorious. Who dares to look on it with unshielded eyes? It has a name in every language. Every child lisps it among his first efforts at articulate speech. It enters into all historic records and is the fundamental condition on which all human affairs proceed. Daily familiarity with it deadens the impression it naturally makes; but could some adult man see it for the first time in its unclouded mid-day brilliancy, or pavilioned amid its sunset glories, he would think no other visible object worthy of note in comparison—could perhaps be easily persuaded by

Satan to think it Deity Himself and fall down
before it in worship, as thousands have done.
Alas !

If the moon is queen of the night, certainly the
sun is king of the day. No other king ever blazed
away so gloriously in barbaric pearl and gold.
Brighter than anything else known to us ; several
times brighter than lightning itself ; brighter than
all other celestial objects if packed together—it is
a fitting symbol of the final glory of the redeemed,
of the present glory of the holy angels, and even
of the eternal glory of the Lord. So think the
Holy Scriptures. And they know.

This most imposing monarch outshines as much
in usefulness as in glory. Were it not for the sun
we should not have the currents that now do so
much to keep our air and waters in a healthy
state. Were it not for the sun all the beautiful
colors that are seen in Nature would be wanting ;
for it paints the blueness of the sky, the greenness
of the fields, the endless hues of flowers and birds
and leaves and gems, and even the mingled lily
and rose on the cheek of beauty. Were it not for
it the earth might become a knight errant, and go
off romancing into the depths of space, colliding
with and dashing in pieces other worlds and itself
also. Were it to withdraw its beams the pall

of perpetual night would settle on the whole world; years and seasons and days would cease their grateful round ; the earth would shiver as it darkened, would stiffen as it shivered, would become frozen stone to its very core, and not all the forests that clothe its surface nor coals and oil that hide within could keep it from becoming a dead world. We ourselves would disappear if the sun should disappear. I say *disappear*— nothing more.

These are facts. But they have been expanded into fictions by some who have spoken and written in the name of science. We are told that not only is the substance of the earth derived from the sun, but that all terrestrial life is generated by it, and even that all our intellectual and moral powers and activities, all our philosophy and poetry and statesmanship and science and even religion itself, are contained potentially in its beams.

To put it mildly, this is pernicious nonsense. Life and mind are not the product of solar forces. The sun is not a creator. It is merely the *condition* of our activity and life in this world. It is that without which beings constituted as we are could not long continue to work, or even to exist as living bodily structures. That is all. And that is a very different thing from saying that "the sun is the ultimate source of all vegetable and animal life and even of the phenomena of mind." This latter means materialism, and materialism in the end means atheism.

This very useful, but by no means divine, luminary has from remote times been supposed to be far more remote from us than is the moon. An ancient astronomer inferred this from the position of the two bodies in respect to each other at the time of the half moon. But the actual distance of the sun from us is found by means of what is called its parallax. How much is it apparently displaced on the sky by a given change in the place of an observer? The answer to this question amazes us by giving a distance of about 93 millions of miles—a distance so immense that sensation itself could not travel so far during three human generations, and yet not so great but that the sun is able to shoot its luminous arrows across it in eight minutes. With this distance a body appearing as large as the moon must be 800,000 miles in diameter. See one of the many illustrations furnished by astronomy that first impressions are often false impressions! Things often are not what they seem. It is always safe to look at an object twice before making up your mind about it.

Eight hundred thousand miles in diameter! This means a globe that could hold more than a million earths. But this tells us nothing about the relative quantities of matter in the two bodies. How do we know but that the sun is as dense as platinum ? How do we know but that it is as tenuous as hydrogen and so has very little matter in its huge bulk ? We know by comparing the attracting forces of the sun and earth on the same object at the same distance. We find that the sun pulls 350,000 times stronger on the moon than the earth would if equally remote. That settles the matter ; for attraction is directly as the quantity of matter. Though the amount of matter in the sun is so enormous, the average density is only one quarter that of the earth, and yet is considerably greater than that of water. How such a density as this can be maintained in the presence of such ferocious and incalculable heat as belongs to the sun is one of the solar mysteries—and likely to remain so.

The sun holds several such mysteries in its capacious and fervid bosom. Really, the brightest object in the heavens is one of the obscurest. The veil before it is very thick although of fire. It illuminates other things without itself, but nothing within itself. Its floods of beams throw

no light whatever on many of the questions it
suggests. What we find about them is a dense
fog of mutually contradictory speculations which,
however, sometimes venture to call themselves
established science. This is not to be wondered
at : for the sun is the shadow of God. He is a
vast illuminator : our best knowledge comes from
Him ; and yet He remains largely unsearchable
and his ways past finding out.

Let us turn a properly shaded telescope on our
luminary. We find that it always keeps the same
circular bright disc, whatever its situation in
respect to us and so must be a self-luminous globe.
We also notice that the face is not of uniform
brightness but has parts relatively very dark.
These dark spots are seen creeping at a certain
uniform rate across the face in parallel lines ;
which shows that the sun turns round on one of
its own diameters once in twenty-seven days.
But this earthlike rotation brings to the sun no
grateful vicissitude of day and night. Eternal day
reigns yonder—and such a day ! Eternal summer
burns on from age to age, without cessation or
cloud. And such a summer ! This would not
recommend it as a home for such beings as ourselves.

As we continue our watch of the disc an eclipse comes on. The moon creeps in between us and the sun, and at last hides the entire face. Then we see all about the moon's edge a glorious, radiated halo of silver whiteness. This is called the *corona* and shows that we commonly see only a part of the sun ; that like the earth, it has an atmosphere, though of different materials from ours. At the base of the corona and resting on the body of the sun there is seen a zone of scarlet color in a state of vast agitation and some-times tossing itself in jets 300,000 miles high. This zone goes by the name of *chromosphere*, and is thought to consist of clouds of metallic vapor more dense than other parts of the solar atmos-phere. This whole atmosphere is supposed to ex-tend at least half a million of miles beyond the body of the sun as it appears to the eye; and there are not wanting those who stretch the supposition (and suppositions are easily stretched) so far as to say that this atmosphere once extended more than three thousand millions of miles away, and that out of its substance by the mere operation of natural forces and laws the earth and some hun-dreds of other worlds were formed. This suppo-sition has naturally had great favor with atheists as making a God unnecessary to account for

Nature and therefore unphilosophical and unscientific. But there are against it grave astronomical objections, as well as theological, which increase as our knowledge of the heavens increases.

All astronomers agree that the sun is a world on fire after a most tremendous fashion. They differ as to many things ; and many a lance has been broken to shivers over the spots, the faculæ, the solidity, and the original extent of the sun. But that it is the greatest bonfire the world ever saw is universally conceded—provided that nothing festive is understood by the word *bonfire.* None of us would feel like making merry in the immediate neighborhood of such a mighty conflagration. Awe and terror rather than hilarity would possess us. Ah, such oceans and tempests and gehennas of devouring heat ! This might reasonably be inferred from the enormous amount of light and heat that we, at so vast a distance from the sun, receive from it. How it blazes and burns on our tropics and equators? As the intensity of light and heat varies inversely as the square of the distance from the radiant body, at the solar surface it must be great beyond all our power to measure or even conceive. A thermometer that could measure that heat would need to be about as long as the sun is remote. Never was such a furnace !

The sun is in a state of sublime and terrible conflagration in comparison with which the fires that devour our prairies and cities, and leap and roar like triumphing fiends from destruction to destruction are of no account.

As we look at the sun through our shaded telescopes we note many signs of vast commotion. Now and then a spot breaks up with the suddenness of the most sudden thunder clap. Under our eyes the fiery ocean moils and boils and flings itself aloft in surf and breakers and enormous geysers that seem in an agony to get as far as possible into the cooling void. We notice currents that sweep along at the rate of three hundred miles a second—more than ten thousand times the rate of the swiftest earthly winds that so carry everything before them. Never was earthly ocean so lashed into fury by Euroclydons as is that great flaming ocean that we call the sun. And the consequence must be noises almost as terrible as the light and heat. To us, at our distance, the sun is as silent as the grave; the nonconducting emptiness between walls out completely the unspeakable uproar. But at the solar surface that uproar must be enough to kill the living (such living as ours) if not to waken the dead. Such a frenzied maelstrom of thunders and thunderous

groans and shrieks and frightful detonations !—
not all the artillery of the nations and of the
clouds shouting together could make such a prodigious and affrighting outburst of sound.    To the
ear, as well as to the eye, the sun would be a
*Pandemonium.*

Calling to the aid of the telescope the doctrine
of gravitation and the higher mathematics we find
that the sun is even a more restless body than we
have just described.    Not only do its fiery oceans
and atmospheres toss about after the most frantic
fashion, as if tormented in the intolerable fires ;
not only does it rotate so as to wheel its surface
about at the rate of more than 100,000 miles a day,
but we know that it must have very many translatory motions in space.    Some of these motions
are only apparent—as its daily motion about the
earth and its annual motion among the stars eastward, but it has also many real motions which are
carrying it incessantly into new regions never
before visited and never to be visited again.    The
law of gravity requires that in the case of only
two bodies making a stable system both should revolve about their common centre of gravity.    This
centre, in the case of the earth and sun lies far
within the surface of the latter, so that the sun-
centre has only a very small orbit compared with

that of the earth—relatively so small that for most purposes it may be considered no orbit at all. Still it must sometimes be taken into account ; with many corrections on account of other simultaneous motions  For the solar motion is not exactly about the common centre of gravity just spoken of, but about that of three bodies, viz., the sun and earth and moon—not even exactly about this, but about that of the whole solar system; not even exactly about this but about the common gravity centre of all the heavenly bodies, both those we see and those we do not see.  In fine, the sun is moving on an orbit that is the resultant of innumerable attractions and must therefore be sweeping grandly about a centre inconceivably remote. Instead of being fixed, the sun is one of the mightest and most audacious of travellers and explorers, wheeling through the unknown with as much assurance as if following some celestial tramway.  Such tramway, however, would get out of repair, but the law of gravity never.  This law is the right hand with which God drives the chariot of the sun.  It supplies at each moment sure guidance to its rushing and fire-breathing coursers.  So they go safely on their way through the glooms ; never stopping, never hesitating,

4          .

never colliding, never swerving one jot from the will of Him who holds the reins.

What sort of matter is that seething in yon great crucible? The spectroscope tells us that the sun contains several elements that are found in the earth (as iron, zinc, copper, etc); but inasmuch as out of thousands of lines in the solar spectrum only about nine hundred have been referred to known terrestrial substances it looks as though the sun is largely composed of substances not belonging to the earth and so could not be the source from which the sun is derived. The element of oxygen, if it exists at all in the sun, is there in inappreciable amount while it makes not far from one half of the substance of our globe. If our globe had been detached from the sun whose elements are violently seething together in a tremendous stirabout of vapors and gases it would, apparently, have consisted of the same elements in something like the same proportion.

For aught we know there has been no diminuation in the intensity of the fires of the sun within human history or any other history. A failing has been suspected, indeed has been asserted; and some even have gone so far as to say how long it will be before the sun becomes a frozen world.

But this is all speculation, without any foundation in experience and observation. Some countries have grown colder, but others have grown warmer ; and there is no evidence that the earth is now getting from the sun one particle less heat than it received at the remotest geological epoch. What feeds these unfailing fires which blaze away into space with such enormous prodigality? It seems as if there must be supply as well as expenditure. All outgoes and no incomes mean poverty, sooner or later. Some have thought that the heat of the sun is kept up by the constant inrush upon it of meteors. Others think this source of supply quite inadequate, and claim that the sun must be gradually cooling, though as yet imperceptibly, and that the time creeps on when the earth will cease to be habitable on account of the cold and the darkness. They will have it that the world will die by freezing instead of burning. Instead of the 'melting of the elements with fervent heat and the burning up of the earth and the works that are therein,' they maintain that just the opposite event will occur. We had better take the Biblical view—which is also the more scientific, no doubt; though some tell us that the Bible-science cannot be depended on. *They* cannot be depended on.

# IV.

# THE SOLAR FAMILY---I.

RESEMBLANCES.

DIFFERENCES.

ANTIQUITY.

IV.

# THE SOLAR FAMILY—I.

RESEMBLANCES—DIFFERENCES—ANTIQUITY.

When what are commonly called stars are closely watched, certain differences appear among them.
The greater part seem to the naked eye to have
no motion whatever among themselves—only the
regular motion from east to west that is common
to all stars. But others are seen to move about
among the rest ; some of them as if they had lost
their way through the trackless spaces and were
engaged in seeking it after a very irresolute and
zigzag fashion, and of course never finding it.

The chief of these wanderers (*planets* the Greeks
called them) bear the most honorable names that
the ancients could possibly give ; for they are the
names of their highest divinities—Mercury, Venus,
Mars, Jupiter, Saturn, Uranus, Neptune. Besides
these magnates, there are already known to us
about four hundred smaller nomads called *asteroids;*
also a very large number of cloud-like, spectral
bodies which, under the names of comets and

meteors make swifter motions along the sky than any other heavenly bodies. All these bodies, and probably some others not discovered, are sharply distinguished from other stars by the large apparent changes in place that they undergo in a short time.

Now this could not be unless all these vagrants were nearer to us and to one another than to the other stars. They must be our nearest neighbors. They, with the earth, must make a group of celestial islets in the great ocean of space—a group separated by vast wastes from other stars. And the sun itself must belong to this group or family ; for we have seen that it, too, changes its apparent place among the stars enormously.

I have called this group a *family*. And it deserves the name. Its members are as near to one another on the scale of the heavens as the people living in the same house are to one another on the scale of the earth. The distances between themselves are as nothing compared with those separating them from the fixed stars. Also, they have a common head, strongly resemble one another in important respects, and are bound together by stronger bonds than those connecting them with other stars. In fact they are so bound together that a mishap to one of them would bring all to grief. Blot out one of them and the whole group would stagger like a drunken man, or like the ox on whose forehead has fallen the fatal blow. This, however, is true of the planets only.

I have called the companions of the sun the *solar* family. This I do because the sun is the largest, most conspicuous, and most controlling member of the group—*in loco parentis.* So we name the family after him. If any choose to call him king instead of father, and to call the planets subjects instead of children, we do not object. He does govern right royally, no doubt ; but so do some heads of families who are only foster fathers or even elder brothers. So we may regard him as the father of the family though it was not evolved from him. No doubt the sun is the head of the planetary household and deserves to have it named from himself.

So let me introduce to you the *solar* family— planets, asteroids, comets ; but, first of all, the planets Mercury, Venus, the Earth, Mars, Jupiter, Saturn, Uranus, Neptune. I name them in the order of their distances from the sun.

A question ? Shall I now take up these wander· ing stars in their order, and give the most notable facts in regard to each—speaking successively of such matters as the great heat and rattling pace of Mercury, the "sweetness and light" of Venus as the morning and evening star, red Mars with manifest continents and seas and snowy poles and baby moons, belted Jupiter with disturbed face and huge waist and five well grown sons going and coming and teaching us how to measure the velocity of light, curiously be-ringed Saturn with his family octave, Uranus with his body-guard of children four, Neptune wheeling with three moons through the Siberian frontiers of the system ? Shall I proceed in this ancient and well beaten track—and take the consequences ?

I think not. The consequences would be too formidable—that is too dull for both myself and my reader. Besides, time and space are precious. We have to proceed *currente et ardente calamo,* if we proceed at all. So we will try another plan—one that perhaps will not bristle so much with those long astronomical numerals, measurements, and statistics that repel so many, are so unmeaning to most, and are steeped in sunsets or sunrises to nobody.

Almost every family has some features that are common to all its members. We call them *family traits.* It is sometimes hard to tell what it is that makes the family likeness which yet we easily recognize. Is it the size of the eye, or the color of the hair, or the height of the forehead, or the width of the mouth, or is it a peculiar expression made up of all these ? We may not be able to say ; we may only know that there is something running through all the family membership that makes it possible for us to exclaim, off hand, when we see a member, *There goes a Bourbon !*

But in the case of the solar family we find no difficulty whatever in particularizing the family traits. They are easily seen and stated—especially in the case of the planets. Thus, all the planets are worlds in size ; all are globular in form ; all rotate on steadfast axes ; all revolve about the sun in elliptical orbits : all revolve in the same direction and in nearly the same plane ; all are governed in their movements by the same laws and can have their places in the sky at any given moment accurately predicted ; all are non-luminous and shine by the reflected light of the sun. I may as well add, what few scientists will dispute, that all the planets either have been, or are, or will be inhabited by rational and responsible beings.

But in every family, however many the respects in which the members resemble one another, there are other respects in which each is unlike all the rest. Once in a great while twins can be found so nearly alike that a " comedy of errors" naturally results. But such cases are extremely rare. Commonly Antilophus of Ephesus and Antilophus of Syracuse are easily distinguishable from each other. A mere glance is enough to show that it is A that we see and not some other letter of the alphabet. Very seldom indeed have we colorable pretext for asking, " Is it you or your brother ?" If there is any planet that might be a twin brother of the earth it is Mars ; if there is any planet that might be a twin sister of the earth it is Venus ; but no observer, looking at these worlds from the highways of space, would be in any danger of mistaking one of them for either of the others. Much less would there be danger of confounding either of these with the other planets—so great are the differences between them.

Variety in unity—such is the astronomical law. Differences cropping out of uniformities and agreements show themselves liberally among the members of the solar family. They differ in size : which ranges from a diameter of about 3000 miles in the case of Mercury to one of 85,000 in the case of Jupiter. They differ in distance from the sun ; which ranges from about 35 millions of miles in the case of Mercury to nearly 3000 millions of miles in the case of Neptune. They differ in time

of revolution about the sun ; which ranges from
about three months in the case of Mercury to 165
years in the case of Neptune. They differ in
density ; which ranges from that of lead in the
case of Mercury to that of cork in the case of
Saturn. They differ in the number and size of
their moons—a number that ranges from zero (so
far as we yet know) in the case of Mercury and
Venus to eight in the case of Saturn ; and a size
that ranges from tiny globes of from five to fifty
miles in diameter in the case of Mars to globes
almost as large as Mars himself in the case of
Jupiter and Saturn.

In consequence of the difference in distance
from the sun, the planets differ exceedingly in the
amount of light and heat they receive. This
amount ranges from about ten times what the
earth receives in the case of Mercury to about a
three-hundredth part of what the earth receives in
the case of Neptune. Think of a planet ten times
hotter than our hottest summers! Think of a
planet three hundred times colder than our coldest
winters ! This thought has caused some to question whether it is possible that there are inhabitants in at least the extremes of our system. But
why should it be a question ? We ought only to
say that living beings at these extremes must

either be differently constituted from ourselves, or
they must have sources of light and heat independent of the sun—neither of which things is incredible or even unlikely. The earth has in itself no
small stores of heat and light ; Neptune may
contain far more and Mercury far less. Besides,
how unlikely it is that an almighty Creator should
make all living rational beings of one pattern !
Vigorous and sportive life abounds in Arctic colds
and equinoctial heats in which you and I would
speedily perish.

Sometimes a large family has a member greatly
different from all the rest. He is so different as
to excite wonder. He has a certain vein of family
likeness ; but then on the whole what heights and
depths of unlikeness in features, in figure, in disposition, in taste, in moral and mental endowments
of many sorts ! Perhaps he is admirable Crich-
ton ; perhaps almost a Caliban. In either case he
is an astonishment, considering his surroundings.
How could such parents have such a child ! How
could such a child have such brothers and sisters !
He is like a bowlder around which geologists
gather and say *It does not belong here.*

Two members of the solar family differ from
the rest after this huge fashion. These are the
sun and Saturn. The sun is a glowing furnace, a

glorious bonfire ; the only one in the system. Saturn is a world surrounded by a curious assemblage of rings ; the only such world we know in our system, or in any other. *A strange object*, said the first telescope. The latest telescope says the same. Saturn is still a first-class mystery. He looks like a foreigner, a *lusus naturæ*. He is the show member of the family to astronomical beginners. He has drawn more fire from telescopes, from speculations, and from popular lectures than has any other member, excepting the sun himself. And truly that series of concentric rings, hanging in everlasting equilibrium, rotating about the planet, spanning its evening vault with their broad, lustrous baldrics. behind which come and go eight moons in all stages of phase from crescent to full, must make the night of Saturn one that cannot be matched for varied and glorious splendor on any other planet. The Greeks called him CHRONOS and thought him a monster. Let us call and think him a TE DEUM of the heavens, an oratorio of the night, one of the many wonderful creations of Him who knows how to diversify worlds as well as the forms of organic life.

Some families pride themselves on their antiquity. They have been conspicuous and influential for generations, perhaps for centuries. Perhaps they came over in the Mayflower ; perhaps they came over with William the Conqueror ; perhaps they are Howards or Hohenzollerns or Romanoffs, almost claim never to have been otherwise. What a long and shining chain of descent it is that we follow back till the golden links dim and disappear in prehistoric darkness ; and how the link of to-day congratulates itself that so many goodly predecessors bind it to the remote past ! But, looking upward, we see in the solar family an antiquity that defies competition. There may be older things in the heavens (indeed, on reflection I know that there are), but not on the earth. Who knows when that celestial family began ? Its leading members have had names time out of mind. No doubt the many members of the family discovered within the last century have been in their places as long as any. Though we cannot tell exactly how long a time that involves, we know that some greatly antedate the human family itself ; for we have learned that the earth and sun were in existence an indefinite stretch of ages before man appeared. Some geologists have tried, in a rude way, to compute this stretch from the strata of the earth ; some astronomers have tried, in a ruder way, to find out how long it would take to ripen, in a way of natural law, an immense

cloud of gases and vapors into a system of solid
worlds. All give us very formidable figures.
Hundreds of millions of years slip easily from
tongue and pen. But oh, the mighty disagree-
ment between the computers ! Of course these
men are guessers. What they know, and all that
they know, is that the solar family was in existence
ages and ages before the human generations began to march from that first pair to the 1400 millions now spread over the earth. This we do
know. And the antiquaries who go into raptures
over a piece of old furniture, or over a broken tool
dug from the dust heaps of the first Troy, or over
the torso of a winged lion unearthed from Birs
Nimroud, and who say as they touch it with
reverent finger, *How very old this is, and what an experience it has had!* may find something still more
worthy of their antiquarian enthusiasm by gazing
aloft at that old, old solar family which God made
"in the beginning."

This ancient family above us which has never
run out, which has never been broken up by
attacks from without nor by dissensions within,
differs greatly in one respect from old human
families. Its antiquity is that of the individuals
composing it. Human families may have lasted
long, but the individuals at any time composing

5

them have lasted but a short time. " One generation goeth and another generation cometh." It is
only the succession that endures. But in the solar
family it is the individual that goes on and on so
wonderfully. The same wandering stars that first
attracted human notice are wandering above us
still. The same flaming eyes that look down
nightly on us looked down on the " garden eastward in Eden" and on the long succession of
brute animals and plants that preceded it.

Celestial Antiquities, we salute you, and through
you most reverently that Ancient of Days from
whom you came, on whose errands you go, and of
whom you are the faint shadows !

# V.

# THE SOLAR FAMILY.—II.

FUTURE.

HARMONY.

HISTORY.

## V.

# THE SOLAR FAMILY.—II.

FUTURE—HARMONY—HISTORY.

The solar family has had a long past. I will not side with one guesser and say that the long past is ten millions of years, nor with another guesser and say that it is 200 millions of years. But this I can say—the past is long, very long.

But what about the future of the solar family? Is that also long, very long?

Past longevity does not necessarily argue longevity to come. It may even argue death at the door. So astronomers have not failed to ask anxiously about the future of our celestial household. Are there any signs of decay about it? Is there anything answering to gray hairs and wrinkles and bent forms and tottering steps?

Nothing of the sort has yet been noticed. For aught we can see the eye of lovely Venus is not getting dim, nor is the natural force of swift Mercury abating. There is no evidence from records that any of their companions have ever shone more brilliantly, or gone on their way more vigorously than they are doing now. So far as observation and history go theirs is a case of immortal youth.

Not only do astronomers generally admit this, but they think that they have found by close study of the constitution of the family that it contains in itself no seeds of decay. It was framed for perpetuity. Nothing in its structure hinders it from going on forever. La Place has the chief honor in proving by his magnificent mathematics the intrinsic stability of the System of the World. Will the system, then, always remain as it is at present? We cannot say that. Is there an ether diffused through the planetary spaces the natural effect of which, however attenuated, must be to retard the motion of the planets and at last to bring them all together in frightful concussion and ruin? Has that Almighty Will that first organized the solar system, and that still besets it behind and before and lays his hand upon it—has this Almighty Governor no plan for setting the system aside, sooner or later?

God has a plan for burning up the *earth*, even to the point of complete dissolution ; but that this earthly dissolution will extend to other worlds we do not know. " The heavens shall pass away with a great noise and the elements shall melt with fervent heat and the earth and the works that are therein shall be burned up." This shows what is sure to happen, some day, to our world and its atmospheric envelope. But the same divine power that miraculously turns even the rocks into flaming gases can, if it chooses, fend off that flame from our companion worlds. Besides, conflagration and dissolution are not extinction ; and during the whole fiery process by which the earth will be rejuvenated into the new heavens and new earth in which shall dwell righteousness, from first to last the earth may have been holding its place and going its rounds without at all endangering the other members of the family. The household is still entire though one member is sick and under thorough treatment. At last recovery will be complete. When this will be we do not know ; we only know that it will be in connection with the final judgment. Whether that will be to-morrow, or some 365,000 years hence, let him who knows tell.

This vast longevity in the past, and possibly in the future, is the more remarkable on account of the exceeding restlessness of all the members of the solar family. In this respect it is very unlike most long-lived families. These have rested every night.   They have rested one day in seven. Also, they have thrown in a holiday, every now and then, for good measure.  So they have been well preserved.  But nervous, restless, flighty people ; people always in motion and hurry, are apt to wear out soon.  They are always on the way to exhaustion and break-down.

"A rolling stone gathers no moss."  If this is so, those rolling stones that make up the solar family will never be well-to-do.  They are always on the go.  They are never still—no, not for a single minute.   They are rolling on their axes, they are rolling about one another, they are rolling about the sun, and as they roll they are ever courteously making bows more or less profound to one another and to all the shining stars.   And this is not all : for, as we have seen, the sun himself cannot be quiet one single moment.   It is safe to say that, long as he has been in existence, he never could have been found twice in the same place.  The place where he is to-day is not the place where he was yesterday, nor is it the place where it will be to-morrow.   A long good-bye to all three places : he will never see either of them again, *never*.   The fact is he has no fixed home.  If "three removes are as bad as a fire" then he is badly off indeed ; for never did so incorrigible a nomad roam Scy-

thian steppes or Arabian deserts. He is running a
lightning express day and night, absolutely without stops, carrying with him the whole solar family
on a sublime curve whose centre is itself constantly moving. Is it not a little strange that such a
perpetual motion of a family that never takes a
vacation, or a Sabbath, or even a night's rest, has
lasted so long without sign of wear or tear ?

"Not so very strange," the fathers said. "Consider what a roomy house this solar family lives in
—a house so large that each member has plenty of
elbow room, can air his peculiarities freely, need
not interfere with the business or the whims of
any other. Even enemies could manage to live
together in a house 6000 millions of miles in
diameter." And they went on to tell of a vast
crystal dome to which all the fixed stars are
fastened, far outside of all the planets and completely roofing them in. Under this glorious
spangled roof dwell all the solar family from age
to age. In so spacious house the inmates could
move about after a very free and independent
fashion without much risk of damaging collisions
or even unpleasant friction. If anybody had
questioned the reality of this crystal palace a few
centuries ago he would have been unanimously
cast out of the synagogue of science. But now

this old notion of Ptolemy, which was held as good science almost down to our time, has not a single supporter—a fact that assures us that even a unanimous acceptance of a notion by scientists by no means demonstrates it.

No, "the house I live in" of the sun and planets and asteroids and comets is no house at all. It is not even a tent. Those celestials are strictly out-of-door people. "Thank the gods," said certain Germans to Cæsar, "we have never slept under cover since we were born." So all the solar family might say. More than this : they cannot even claim a fixed locality. Of all travelers, even in this traveling age, these are the ones most persistently "not at home" : in fact you never can find them where they last were. But still it is true that the constantly shifting region occupied by the solar family always remains very large, no member of the household ever approaching another within thirty millions of miles, and most of them separated from their fellows by a vastly greater space. If they had been as compactly placed as one can imagine, they would have been far more likely to interfere with one another and so come to grief.

No doubt the immense intervals between its members has something to do with the stability of the solar family. But this stability comes still more from another fact, viz., the essential harmony that exists between its members.

We have excellent authority for saying that "the contentions of brothers are like the bars of a castle" ; also the best of observation proves that such contentions not seldom occur. Brothers and sisters fall out with one another : parents and children wrangle and separate. The same roof can no longer cover them. But the solar family is thoroughly harmonious within itself : harmony is built into its very structure! This is the great reason why its members get on so quietly together —the planets never having been known to collide with one another during the long past, or even to threaten to do so. The meteoric clouds belonging to the system do indeed sometimes rub against the earth ; but they are such shadowy and unsubstantial things that the only result is a shower of shooting stars, more or less brilliant. The earth plows its foamy way through them without any damage whatever to itself and without the least perceptible abatement of its speed. Such collisions count for nothing. The family can stand any number of them.

The planets do not even threaten to harm one another—to one who knows their habits. Their orbits alternately contract and expand ; and when one, year after year, gets nearer and nearer to the sun the situation naturally seems alarming to the uninitiated.    But the astronomer now knows that there is no danger.    The contraction of the orbit has a limit.   "Thus far shalt thou go and no farther."    After a few thousand years the mighty curve begins to swell out to its old dimensions. Its very elasticity, instead of being a threat, is a pledge of safety.    Like the trees of the forest it finds endurance in elasticity, in knowing when to yield somewhat to pressure. Men and institutions, also, have sometimes saved much by yielding a little.

What, at first view, seem to be family jars in the solar family are not so.    The pullings in different directions that we notice are not oppositions but attractions.    Some who have studied the matter closely have found out that the members of the solar family are so attached to one another that they have come under bonds not only never to al- low differences to proceed to extremities in down- right quarrels, but never to *have* any differences. What go by that name are only the friendly hand- pullings that would fain bring lip to lip.    They are a family safety valve or balance wheel that contributes to the general steadfastness.    Is not health the equilibrium of seemingly opposing forces ?

Some one has said that nothing so helps to keep the peace between neighbors as a wall ten feet high. If this is so, we may allow that there is a certain element of peacefulness and harmony in the vastness of the intervals between the planets. But the great cause, I am inclined to think, lies in the fact that the Builder of the solar system so built harmony into its make-up that all the members are obliged to refer disputes, or what seem such, to the sun for arbitration. They have great respect for him : his decisions are final. They know how to obey the head of the family—a kind of knowledge that all minors do not possess. And he knows how to rule, and how to obey Him who rules over all—a kind of knowledge which all heads of families unfortunately do not possess.

The history of the solar family is one thing ; the history of our knowledge of that family is another thing. Doubtless every feature of that first history, down to the minutest incident, has recorded itself somewhere in the universe, and is decipherable from the material tablet on which the laws of light and gravity and other forces have faithfully written it ; but *we* cannot read this self-registered history. Some, however, claim that they have done so to a considerable extent, and proceed to tell us that the family began in an immense fire-cloud extending far beyond the orbit of Neptune : that this cloud in cooling began to revolve about its centre ; that this revolution in the process of cooling at length became so rapid as to detach a nebulous ring ; that this ring in time broke up and condensed into one or more planets which in some cases also threw off rings which condensed into moons ; that the ever increasing speed of rotation in the fire-cloud kept repeating this process until now we have many planets, and the original cloud by successive losses of its substance is reduced to the observed size of the sun. Then, turning to geology, they proceed to confirm and continue this history by showing that our earth, taken as a sample of the other members of the family, passed gradually in immense stretches of time from at least a fused state to the humbler forms of vegetable life and then to the humbler forms of animals, and so on until at last we have man and the earth as it now is. " From one learn all," they say. " Here you have the history of the solar family."

The objections to this supposed history are of two sorts. First are certain facts within the system itself; such as the great ellipticity of some

of the orbits, the great inclination of some of the
orbits to the solar equator, the retrograde motion
of some of the comets and moons, the relation
as to velocity between the sun's rotation and the
revolutions of some of the planets, also between
the rotations of some of the planets and the revolutions of their moons—Mars furnishing a notable example.

These and many more such difficult facts make
one sort of objection. Another sort is of a still
graver character, viz., that the hypothesis if true,
sets aside the argument from design in the works
of Nature for the being of a God. Stated plainly
in one form it teaches that Nature is a natural
growth from the humblest beginnings, that worlds
and their organic forms have slowly come up
from exceedingly simple things by purely natural causation. Such at least is the understanding
of the hypothesis by its leading advocates. This
is the understanding to the establishment of which
all their efforts are directed. They insist on a
natural genetic connection between any two con-
secutive variations in that long series of small
variations by which things are supposed to have
crept up from the simplest structures or from
elementary atoms to their present state.

But whatever be the force that actually conducts Nature slowly upward along the succession of minute steps, whether it be natural or supernatural, if these steps are such and so minute that merely natural forces *can* easily take them, then proof of a God must come from some other quarter than from what we have been used to call his works. Yet, the Bible says, "The invisible things of Him from the creation of the world are clearly seen being understood by the things that are made even his eternal power and godhead so that they (the heathen) are without excuse." But they are not without excuse if the earth and heavens have been built in such a way that not even a philosopher can tell whether Nature built itself or was built by God.

# VI.

# THE SOLAR FAMILY.—III.

## SUPERSTITIONS.

## VI.

# THE SOLAR FAMILY.—III.

### SUPERSTITIONS.

Great and old families are apt to have some superstitions connected with them. Some room in the castle is haunted ; some wicked or unfortunate or uncomfortable ancestor walks ; certain dates or generations in the family history are critical and need watching. There is hardly an historic family that has not some superstitions of this sort hanging about it.

The solar family is no exception. It wheels into line, and at the head of the line. Spectres, portents, lucky and unlucky aspects, *dies fasti et nefasti*, mysteries of Udolpho and Otranto—they have all somehow managed to domesticate themselves in the blue dome above.

I have already noticed some widely spread superstitions about the moon; and there are many others. For example we are told that the moon has a powerful influence on health, on the complexion, on the weather, on the mind in producing

or modifying insanity, on the proper times of
planting and reaping and felling timber and
killing domestic animals. Some things must be
done in the old of the moon, some things in the
new, and some in the full. Country people have
heard that medicinal herbs gathered when the
moon increases have the most virtue; that cucum-
bers grow best at full moon, while onions do best
in the moon's decline; that vines trimmed at
night, when the moon is in Leo, will be most
likely to escape field rats and other gnawing animals.

From time out of mind such notions about our
satellite appear to have prevailed widely among
all classes, not excepting philosophers and scientists. The first lunar tables computed according
to the Newtonian theory of gravity were intended
for astrological purposes; and the weather alma-
nacs, of which a few survive, were the practical
science of such journals as the *Connaisance des Temps*
less than two hundred years ago. Mortifying, is
it not? Science has sometimes stooped before
conquering.

But the moon is not the only member of the
solar family that has been saddled with a great
double pack of superstitions. Fortunately she
has been able to hold on her way with unabated

pace notwithstanding the unreasonable load. Some
even say that all the while she has been going
faster. I have no doubt they are right. But all
along she had the encouragement of good and
sympathizing company. Every one of the planets, except those lately discovered, has had a like
burden to carry and has carried it equally well.
Uranus and Neptune had a great escape by keeping in the dark as long as they did. Astrology
would have kept them hard at work predicting
the fates of men who, for the most part, were
beneath their notice.

See how the ages, until lately, have been talking
about the older planets ! I say *until lately;* but
even now, in our metropolitan newspapers, the
advertisements of astrologers may sometimes be
found. For a dollar or so, one may learn whether
or not the planets smiled on his birth ; also when
the critical times of his life may be expected.
But the superstitions that now lurk only in cor-
ners, and shady ones at that, only a little while
ago walked the whole earth in broad day and
robes of honor, bowled along boulevards in char-
iots of bronze, and lifted unabashed front in the
halls of learning and the councils of kings. No
great enterprise was undertaken without consulting the planets. No one ventured to open his

lips against this science of the day. Did not even the Bible confirm it—the Bible that says, " The stars in their courses fought against Sisera ?"

Each planet was supposed to influence the fortunes of men according to the times of their births. If Jupiter was in the first sign of the Zodiac at the birth, the child would have high station ; if Mars, his career would be violent and quarrelsome ; if Venus, he would be favored in the matter of accomplishments and love ; if Mercury, he would be ingenious and cunning, perhaps eloquent and learned. Mars was thought to be a very unlucky planet to be born under; but Saturn was the unluckiest of all. Nothing but misfortune for the child that happened to be born under its influence ! If at that time the planet chanced to be in the zodiacal sign of the month, the very worst sort of a career was to be expected for the youngster. He was foreordained to disaster, and oceans of it. Parents threw up their hands in despair. Nothing could be done for him. Hope forsook him, and of course every thing else did.

Just think of it ! Such baseless notions as these were held almost unchallenged for thousands of years, among the most scholarly and enlightened, from far beyond the time when in Egypt and Chaldea astrologers were a standing part of the equipment of governments! All in the name of the highest science too! We are ashamed to confess it—but facts are stubborn things. And we must bow to the stubbornness of facts. It is some consolation to know that Joseph and Daniel belonged to a different order of wise men from that which divined by the stars.

"We open here a new budget," as says the Chancellor of the Exchequer—the budget of the eclipses. It is only yesterday, as it were, when the general public of the best countries came to know that eclipses of the sun were caused by the moon coming in between us and the sun, and eclipses of the moon by its passing through the earth's shadow. For untold stretches of years before, they passed for heavenly predictions of earthly disaster, for tokens of divine wrath and banners of advancing judgment on princes and peoples. Especially was this idea held about total eclipses of the sun. These totals have been wont to set mankind aghast. "A dragon is eating up the sun," said savages; and they tried to drive the monster away with shouts and various din. "Heaven is angry with us for our sins, and warns the Son of Heaven to look up his faults and correct them," said the Chinese chief mandarin; and the whole empire prostrated itself and remains prostrate till now. And in more classic countries, from the time of Nicias in Sicily and of Alexander at Arbela down to times that have hardly yet gone below the horizon, seditions have been quelled, defeats suffered, victories won, governments unsettled, whole nations sent to their knees by such signs of divine wrath. No doubt the wrath was real; for the ages have been awfully wicked— only the eclipses were no proof of the wrath. But there were other proofs and plenty of them. The universal consciousness of guilt is itself enough to set the heavens aflame, much more to eclipse all the stars.

"A spirit passed before my face; the hair of my flesh stood up." Not long ago the hair of almost everybody was as electrical as that of Eliphaz the Temanite. They saw a spirit among the stars. What else could it be—that weird and ghostly thing that had so suddenly appeared in the sky with the fierce face and snaky tresses of Tisiphone!

From time to time men have looked up and seen a hazy object with a starlike nucleus and a streamer extending a long distance. What was it? It looked spectral—a ghostly monster bent on ravage and ruin, and moving among the stars at a furious pace and with a ferocious aspect. Is it not a messenger from an angry God to announce hastening judgments? The phantom in itself was sufficiently grim: and it was easy for people always haunted by the consciousness of guilt to fancy additional terrors in its aspect. Curious pictures have come down to us from the Middle Ages of comets as they seemed to the terrified vision of the time. Cruel malevolence, savage ferocity, vindictive hate, fiendish mockery, outrageous passion, stark and raving insanity—all were depicted or attempted in those rude representations, half ludicrous and wholly horrible. The pictures are no photogrophs. The eye gave the outlines; a terrified imagination did the rest. And what a painter a frightened imagination is!

The rest was indeed frightful. No wonder the people feared the worst. No wonder that the vulgar went wild. Pestilence and war on a great scale were at hand. Everything bad was knocking at the door of the nations. Thrones would topple, armies would sink in bloody graves. Death on the pale horse of the plague or famine or earthquake would ride forth on his fearful errand. The hair of nations stood up. Their knees smote together. Cold, clammy sweat stood on their brows. Men's hearts failed them for fear and for looking after the things that are coming on the earth. What terror-smitten faces were turned up to the portentous stranger of 1680 from cabins and halls and castles and palaces—from under the matted hair of serfs, the plumed hats of gentry, the serge cowls of monks, the steel morions of soldiers, and the jeweled crowns of kings! It means you, O oppressive and voluptuous monarch! It means you, O subjects imbruted, and God-defying! Those who were not dismayed at the heavenly sign were counted hardened sinners who could reasonably be taken in hand by the magistrate.

Thus it was for many weary centuries. Here and there a man, like Seneca, held juster views: and indeed juster views were also held by the early Chaldean and Greek astronomers. But then came a great scientific backsliding which lasted for millenniums. What! scientists mistaken! What! scientists almost or quite unanimous in the mistake and for so long a time, too! Yes, we must confess it, though very reluctantly. Religion has no monopoly of backsliding. The same science that fell from grace and the Pythagorean view of the solar system into the Ptolemaic, and remained fallen so long, soon fell away from the true view of comets and lay quite as prostrate as the general public. From the birth of Christ some five hundred comets have been recorded: and in regard to most of them observers of every grade have, until lately, had but one opinion. They were thought supernational visitors. They were either the inflictors or the prophets of divine judgments. Nobody thought that they meant nothing or meant good. Everybody thought they meant evil, and evil on a great scale—public disaster, ruin to monarchs, kingdoms, continents. Of course this thought still remains among hundreds of millions who are still barbarous or semi-civilized.

See how the celebrated surgeon, Ambroise Paré, describes the comet of 1528. "This comet was so horrible and dreadful that it engendered such great terror to the people that they died, some with fear, others with illness. It appeared to be of immense length and of blood color; at its head was seen the figure of a curved arm holding a large sword in its hand, as if it wished to strike. At the point of the sword were three stars, and on either side were seen a great number of hatchets, knives, and swords covered with blood, among which were numerous hideous human faces with bristling beards and hair."

But perhaps no comet is responsible for so much consternation as Halley's. It has appeared twenty-four times during the Christian era. Of its appearance in 837 a French writer wrote thus: "During the holy days of Easter a phenomenon ever fatal and of gloomy forebodings, appeared in the heavens." It was supposed to predict the death of Louis le Debonnaire, which took place shortly after.

Its appearance in 1066, when the Normans invaded England, was supposed to predict the defeat and subjection at the disastrous battle of Hastings. In 1455 it appeared again. At that time the Turks were threatening Europe. Constantinople had been taken by storm and the siege of Belgrade raised. Pope Calixtus III., summoned the chivalry of Europe to arms. The Mohammedan East and the Christian West stood confronting each other with lifted scimetars and battle axes. The embattled hosts looked up and saw the comet. Whose ruin did it portend? To make all sure the pontiff fulminated a bull against the comet and bespoke its curses for the enemy. The enemy got them. In the great battle that followed the crescent lost and the cross won. Europe was saved.

At last, and quite too late, our astronomy has shown that such notions in regard to comets are mere superstitions. We can look up with great composure, though not without great interest, on the most truculent looking celestial phantom that ever frightened the nations. We now know that these Eumenides are nothing but masses of cloud-like matter belonging to the solar family; masses so extremely tenuous that if they should rush into the earth we should suffer no disturbance beyond what a brilliant display of shooting stars would make.

The comets move in calculable orbits about the sun according to the same laws that govern the planets; and the times of their returns to us have often been foretold with great exactness. The very constitution of some of them when in a state of incandescence has been found by means of the spectroscope, and found to consist of not more than three gases, mostly carbon and hydrogen. Also, the various aspects and movements that they show, are, in the main, such as masses of extremely tenuous matter circulating about the sun in extremely elliptical orbits would necessarily show. They become visible only when near the sun; when first visible through the telescope they are mere cloudlets of uniform appearance; as they come nearer to us in their advance towards the sun they brighten more and more, move faster and faster, show central condensation more and more clearly, and their substance gradually expands into streamers, sometimes of enormous length, through which the faintest stars can be seen. As they retreat from the sun this order is reversed, and the prodigal sons, as usual, come out at the little end of the horn.

All this is what we should expect of misty cloudlike matter in course of circulation about the sun on very eccentric orbits. Comets are fellows of the planets, children of the same solar family; or at least its life-long domestics and feudal retainers. Though unsubstantial children of the mist they obey the laws of gravity, respect the three famous statutes of Kepler, and submit to the central authority of the sun as well as do the most solid members of the shining household.

It is true that in some respects besides their unsubstantial character the comets are very unlike the planets. To all appearance they are the flighty, erratic, dissipated vagabonds of the system —its prodigal sons, ever dashing away on their mighty sprees to far countries and at last returning with inflamed faces and dishevelled hair and tattered garments toward the father's house. The cometary orbits lie at all angles to ours, and are generally so extremely eccentric as to subject them to wonderful extremes of temperature and motion—facts not easily explained on the nebular hypothesis. The comet of 1843, for example, almost brushed the sun with its fiery tresses, and then, as if in mortal terror at its audacity, rushed away at the rate of 1,200,000 miles an hour toward the frozen regions far beyond the orbit of Neptune, where its pace is only a few yards an hour. Despite the proverb, such extremes never meet. They are like the extremes of some erratic Christians—now very hot and now very cold, now very fast and now very slow, now very near the Sun and now so far away that it seems as if they would never get back; and yet real members of the household of faith and bound to return, though it be in a very shattered and tattered condition.

The comets are subject to various diversities and changes of aspect which have not as yet been explained. The ideal comet, when in full parade uniform and well behaved,—appears with a bright, eyelike nucleus in a hairy envelope from which streams out a prodigious pennon or tail. But comets do not always appear in parade dress. They are not always well behaved. Sometimes they omit the bright cyclopean eye, sometimes the hazy envelope, sometimes the tail; and the tail when present appears in very different forms. Now it is straight, now curved, now like a fan more or less opened, now like a sword, now like a giant club. now like the long dishevelled and storm-tossed tresses of a classical Fury. Sometimes all these varieties appear in the same comet during successive trips about the sun; for example, in Halley's comet in its returns in 1456, 1682, 1759, 1835. The head of a comet has been known to split asunder as if by the axe of some invisible Vulcan, though no wise goddess ever appeared as the result.

We cannot as yet well explain these strange behaviors; which have done much to promote superstitious fears. Speculations have been plentiful enough; but as yet science has been invoked in vain. But this is not disturbing. Rather it is stimulating. It is after the historic manner of our progress in the knowledge of nature. Satisfactory explanations, will be reached by and by after much sifting and winnowing. Oh for a wind just strong enough to blow away the chaff and leave the wheat! Methinks I hear it rising now. Soon it will be here. And meanwhile we see clearly that there is a great difference between the unexplained, and even the unexplainable, and the supernatural.

Do I deny that comets are supernatural? By no means. Nature itself is supernatural.

# VII.

# THE SOLAR FAMILY—IV.

## INHABITANTS?

## VII.

# THE SOLAR FAMILY—IV.

INHABITANTS.

*Are the planets inhabited?*

I suppose that most astronomers are inclined to answer this question in the affirmative as to some of the planets; and that they would say in regard to all of them that they either are, or have been, or will be, the abodes of living beings.

The reasons for this guarded statement are found in the history of our own planet. Geology shows that there was a long time during which no living beings existed on the earth—a time in which the earth was only in course of preparation as a habitation. And our Scriptures tell us that the time will come (apparently a brief one) when the earth will no longer be inhabited. So we who believe in both the Bible and Geology—wholly in the Bible and partly in Geology—are not prepared to affirm that all the planets are, just now, the homes of living beings. They may be, and they may not be. We see no valid ground for maintaining that they are at this moment unoccupied by rational and responsible beings. But all that we affirm is that they were made to be inhabited at some time.

As yet we have no instruments that can look in upon even the nearest planet so as to discover such beings as men, or their works, if they exist there. The time may come when we can do this, and some think that it is even now at the doors by means of photography; but it has not lifted knocker yet. As yet we cannot recognize any great artificial structures, like pyramids or cathedrals or Grand Centrals, anywhere outside of our own world—much less the builders of such things.

Since, then, we cannot *see* whether there are living beings on the planets, how do we justify ourselves in believing that they are, or have been, or will be, inhabited?

There are several lines of argument. The one I will present is none the worse for having a spice of religion about it.

GOD made all the heavenly bodies. They are not eternal. They did not come by chance, nor by mere natural law. They came at the word of Him who "spake and it was done, who commanded and it stood fast." "In the beginning God created the heavens and the earth."

If God made the planets what did He make them for? Certainly He had an object in view. As certainly this object was one worthy of the outlay to secure it. Did he make these great globes and send them on their glorious rounds about the sun in order to add a few more ornamental points to our evening sky? Was it to exercise the curiosity and patience of a handful of astronomers? The world is at last well recovered from the idea that we are the centre of the universe, and that the stars were made for our benefit, especially so small a benefit. We are more than convalescing from that stubborn distemper of the ages. To us at the present day it goes without saying that the outlay of power and wisdom on the planets is too immense for so paltry an end. What, then, can be the object of the planets?

As to the object of one of them, namely the earth, we have Divine information. "For thus saith the Lord that created the heavens; God himself that formed the earth and made it, he hath established it, he created it not in vain, he *formed it to be inhabited.*" Of course to be inhabited in the way it actually is, by innumerable forms of animal life culminating in rational and moral beings. Man is the chief figure in this comprehensive object.

Other things are relatively worthless. It was, therefore, chiefly for him that the earth was made. Accordingly it is written: "The earth has he given to the children of men."

Now look at our neighbor Mars. It seems almost a duplicate of the earth. Behold land, water, and air! Behold clouds, rains, snows! Behold continents, oceans, lakes! Behold days and seasons and mean temperature very well answering to our own! And then the newly discoverd moons! A map of Mars much resembles a map of the earth in its general features—though with more land than water. There seems no reason why, if our animated tribes could be transferred across the abyss to that next door neighbor of ours, nearly all of them could not have homes assigned them agreeing very well with those they now occupy. How natural to infer that a globe so much like our own was made for a like purpose —made to be inhabited! We do not need to *draw* the inference—the inference draws us. If a certain builder has made two contiguous houses so much alike that one can hardly tell one from the other; and one of them is known to have been meant for a dwelling house, and to be actually occupied as such; how natural and indeed imperative is the conclusion that the other structure is meant for the same purpose—whether at present occupied or not!

Almost as much can reasonably be said of beautiful Venus—the nearest neighbor on the other side of us. Though its surface is not as clear to us as is that of Mars, it is morally certain that it would be equally habitable for terrestrial life.

We have, then, at least three planets which the Creator made to be inhabited. This creates a strong presumption that the object of the other planets—so like to these in great cosmical features and arrangements—is the same. But here some feel a difficulty; best recognized in the case of the two extreme planets, Mercury and Neptune. The one is so near the sun that the mean amount of light and heat which it gets from that luminary is seven times what the earth receives. On the other hand Neptune is so far away from the sun that it receives only about the eight hundredth part of the heat and light that we do. How can life exist under such conditions—the terrible oven on the one hand and the terrible refrigerator on the other! Our answer is that the temperature of a planet and the amount of light it has do not depend solely on its distance from the sun; they also depend much on the sort and depth of its atmosphere; the number, distance, and structure of its moons; the nature of its soil; and especially its amount of internal fires. By changing the condition of the earth as to these matters, as we may suppose it to be changed, we could easily raise or lower its temperature and amount. of light very largely, indeed to almost any extent. So every planet in the system *may* be furnished with climate and light not unsuited to the terrestrial races of living beings.

But why say *terrestrial* races—as if there could be no other forms of living being than such as are found in our world! Who has a right to say either that God could not, or that He would not make beings adapted to live and thrive in widely different physical conditions from our own! Must all living creatures be made after the earthly patterns? Has the Omniscient and Almighty such poverty of resources? Can he not make races that can live and flourish in the airless and waterless moon (we are by no means sure that our moon is so poverty-stricken) as well as we do here—as well even in the furnace of the sun with its thousands of blazing equators as we on our temperate zones? Could He not people worlds with pure spirits, or with beings whose etherial bodies so closely border on the spiritual as to be almost independent of material surroundings?

There is but one answer which a believer in the God of the Bible can give to such questions.

What magnificent bodies some of the remoter planets are? What a glory of magnitude and moons waits on them? Think of Saturn with its wonderful ring and eight moons; together making such an evening sky as never arched the earth. Can it be that the largest and most beautiful worlds in our system were made for a purpose less considerable than our own—that God has framed such palaces for emptiness, or the vegetable, or the worm, while "giving the earth to the children of men!" We answer *No*—in the name of the eternal beauty and fitness of things.

These views are practically universal, not only among Christian astronomers, but among scientists· of all shades of religious opinion. What a waste of power and grandeur if our own little world is the only inhabited one? But it is seen that Nature is not wont to waste herself in this profitless and prodigal fashion; to make this much ado about nothing. Accordingly, even infidels are in the habit of maintaining the plurality of inhabited worlds; and have sought in the fact arms against the Bible. These men are generally radical evolutionists, and so are compelled to say that, inasmuch as all planets have been formed under precisely the same natural laws and in precisely the same manner, their histories must be substantially the same with that of our world—a world that has been pushed forward from one grade of population to another until at last it has reached men.

And yet it is not common in our day for astronomical text books to express any opinion as to the object for which the planets were made. It is thought to be in bad taste. It is thought to be unscientific. Professional scientists are almost as much afraid of mixing up religion with science as professional politicians are of mixing it up with politics. But Sir Isaac Newton did not think it unscientific to acknowledge God and final causes in the very presence of the Calculus. And Sir John Herschel, a man of kindred genius and attainment, did not hesitate to write to young people as follows: "For what purpose are we to suppose such magnificent bodies scattered through the abyss of space? He must have studied astronomy to little purpose who can suppose man to be the only object of his Creator's care, or who does not see in the vast and wonderful apparatus around us provision for other races of animated beings."

But it is time to move on. So good bye to the Solar Family—that large, brilliant, and ancient

family; that family which at first view seems so
vagrant and lawless but which on closer examination turns out to be harmonious and well-behaved
and well-governed in the last degree; never re-
belling, never playing truant, never seriously dis-
obeying the Sun in any respect though all are so
headstrong and flighty by nature and some of them
so eccentric in their bias that if the Sun should not
keep a strong hand on them they would rush away
into all sorts of mischief, carrying with them the
fates of vast populations. But the Sun *does* keep
a strong hand and a steady. The sire is no weak-
ling. He is a miracle of quiet firmness. His
children have to behave themselves. And so quiet
and safety and order reign because subordination
reigns.

# VIII.

# OTHER SOLAR FAMILIES—I.

CREDIBLE.

MANY.

DISTANT.

# OTHER SOLAR FAMILIES—I.

CREDIBLE—MANY—DISTANT.

Is our Solar Family the only one? In all the round of the heavens is there no other sun circled by its own system of dependent worlds?

Some people can see only themselves: and very near-sighted people they are. Others manage to see in addition their own family—nothing more. But there are others who are not content with so narrow a range of vision; who, looking away beyond themselves and their own immediate household, succeed in finding that there are other households, and many of them as important and worthy of attention as their own.

To this last class astronomers belong. They have looked away far beyond their own star, far beyond the family of stars to which they belong, and have found millions on millions of other solar families many of which would seem to be more magnificent than their own.

Of these I will now speak.

Every fixed star is a sun.  If our sun could be carried away from us indefinitely it would lessen and lessen on our sight until at last it would appear like any fixed star—a mere point on the sky, incapable of being magnified by any telescope, and unchangeable in position to any common observation.  This suggests that all the fixed stars may be vast suns belittled to the eye by distance.  But, on examining the quality of their light by the spectroscope and other means, we find the suggestion emphasized into knowledge.  Their light, like that of our sun, is the light of incandescent bodies; and the material that is glowing in them is, to a certain extent, like that which glows in our own luminary.  So it is plain that if any fixed star could be made to approach us it would gradually brighten and expand on our sight until at last it would appear as large as our sun and would affect us similarly as to light and heat.

So all the fixed stars are suns.  Have they planets about them ?

The most eminent astronomers, like Newton and La Place and Arago and Bessel and Struve and the two Herschels, have not hesitated to answer in the affirmative.  I do not know of a single astronomer who maintains a negative.  The considerations weighing with such men are various. Some of the stars, under the best telescopes, appear with minute companions that have been suspected to shine by reflected light. Others show certain delicate disturbances of position such as would be produced by the attractions of near planets. But the great reason, no doubt, lies in the analogy of our own system, and in that sense of the beautiful and fitting that rules in all true scientists, but especially in those believing in a personal God. Such men cannot conceive of any other equally fitting purpose for such bodies. That such immense spheres, as these suns must be that never change their place to common observation, were created merely to decorate our evening sky, is neither believed nor believable at the present day. If they were made to be sources of light and heat and government to schemes of dependent and habitable worlds, the end is worthy of the outlay, and our sense of the eternal beauty and fitness of things is satisfied. Accordingly, there is, probably, not a single astronomer who believes in Him who made the stars who does not also believe that each star is a sun belted with planets designed for habitations. More than this. Even agnostics and atheists are accustomed to regard the stars as representing so many planetary systems. It is a

8

necessary corollary from that nebular hypothesis that is such a favorite with all sorts of unbelievers, but especially with those of the red-republican stamp. "By the laws of Nature," say they, " a sun is the head of a family—is a sire and perhaps a grandsire."

So we are to consider that there are as many Solar Families as there are fixed stars. Each fixed star is a sun and if, like our sun, it is a locomotive world, it masterfully drags after it wherever it goes a train of dependent worlds indissolubly coupled with it and with one another.

How many are they?

The taking of a large census—I mean an accurate one—is no easy matter anywhere, whether in the heavens or on the earth. Say on the earth. The work has to be committed to many persons, some of whom have a genius for accuracy and others a genius for blunders. The districts canvassed sometimes overlap one another and sometimes they fall short. In lonely places, on the borders of towns, some people are overlooked; still more escape notice in the greater loneliness of crowded cities. Crowds are coming and going, streaming this way and that, hiding in garrets and cellars—how can they be surely counted? To be sure one may count the houses, and, with difficulty, the rooms in

them; but how many waifs have no houses or
rooms to shelter them, and, of those who have
something of the sort, how many are unwilling to
report themselves and their miseries! Rather
than enter some pestiferous dens the census-taker
is tempted to guess at their contents, or to take
them on testimony as wide of the mark as drunk-
enness and roguery can make it. So there is
always a margin of uncertainty in the official
returns of population for any large nation. This,
however, we do not mind. Approximations to
truth are sometimes about as good as the truth
itself. In fact we had rather have 3.14159 as
expressing the ratio of the circumference of a
circle to its diameter than to have the same figures
pushed into complete accuracy by the addition to
them of an infinite number of decimals. What
matters a mistake of a few hundreds or thousands
in a census of sixty odd millions!

Like difficulties are found in taking a census of
the fixed stars. The work has to be divided up
among observers in two hemispheres; and it is not
easy to guard against either overlapping or over-
looking. Some observers are patient and careful;
and others are otherwise. We are not troubled
by the stars moving about in all directions, as do
the people in our cities—for it takes very close and

long continued observation to detect in them any motion whatever—still it is a hard matter to count them when they are crowded together, or when they lie on the frontiers of vision. On these frontiers the stars are so faint that we are uncertain whether they are stars at all. So a celestial census, like an earthly, is liable to a certain amount of error. But no matter. A few thousands, or even millions, of stars, more or less, are of little account in estimating the immense celestial populations.

I say *immense.* There can be no question about that. Before telescopes a vague look at the evening sky gave the impression of an innumerable number of bright points: and to-day the same impression is given to the great masses of mankind as they glance upward. And this impression is correct. "As many as the stars of the sky in multitude and as the sands of the sea-shore innumerable," say the Scriptures; and our latest science says the same. For though, on proceeding to individualize the stars visible to the naked eye, we can only make out five or six thousands, on calling the telescope to our aid we find the number greatly enlarged, and the larger the telescope the greater the shining hosts revealed, until now the number within reach of our keenest-eyed instrument is estimated at one hundred millions.

Is this all? Apparently all the stars just mentioned belong to the Milky way, or that particular firmament of stars in which our sun is imbedded; but, all along, every successive advance in the space penetrating power of our instruments has brought to light what seem other firmaments as large and glorious as our own. Have we reached the frontier of the stellar heavens just as our object glasses have reached a diameter of little over three feet? Very unlikely indeed—millions of chances to one against it. If such has been the law of our intercourse with the heavens from the time when Galileo turned his pigmy object-glass on the sky to the present when the Earl of Rosse turns upward his gigantic six feet speculum, are we not entitled to feel that we might still go on indefinitely adding host to hosts? In short we seem forbidden by experience to set limits to the number of the stars—especially since photography has come to the aid of the telescope.

This, then, is our answer to the question. How many Solar Families besides our own? Perhaps one hundred millions distinctly in view; and this the beginning only of the glorious census. For one I have no idea that any arithmetic intelligible to us could write down the mighty total. The universe of suns and worlds is practically and potentially infinite. The ancients were right—the heavens are *full* of eyes. I doubt whether the fleetest and oldest angel ever saw a star beyond which there was no other. I doubt whether there *is* such a star. The universe is GREAT—its Maker only is greater.

How many are the stars? The Science of Number, tablets in hand, ascends the loftiest Nebo of observation furnished by any world and looks abroad over the immensities to take the mighty census. She faces north and south and east and west; she looks upward and downward, near and far. She turns pale. The stylus drops from her trembling fingers. In mingled astonishment and bewilderment she flings her hands heavenward and exclaimes: " Impossible ! This census-taking is infinitely beyond me. Not even my elder sister who dwells among the angels is equal to such a feat as this—only He who made the heavens, and of whose intelligence we sciences are but sparks, can do it. He counteth the number of the stars and calleth them all by their names."

So much for the number of the stars. And we are to bear in mind that this means not merely an incalculable number of spangles on the ebony vault of our night, not merely uncountable bonfires in the frozen wastes of space, not merely so many glorious suns in size and splendor, but so many systems of revolving and habitable worlds. Ahasuerus reigned over a hundred and twenty-seven provinces, and they called him the Great King: what name shall we give to the King whose provinces not even the angels can number, and whose every province is a confederacy of worlds?

Turning from the number of the Solar Families to their distances, we ask:

*How far are they from us and from one another?*

It is only a few years ago when the only possible answer to this question would have been, "They are all more than 200,000 sun-distances from us:" and the answer would have been justified by the fact that if any star were nearer to us than this its apparent place on the sky would be changed one second of arc, by our passing through half of the earth's orbit. So large a displacement had not then been found. Nor has it been found since. But since then better instruments and better methods have enabled us to recognize smaller displacements—first in the star called *61 Cygni*, and afterward in several other stars. The nearest of these, *Alpha Centauri* is more than 18 billions of miles away from us—a distance so great that light, traveling at the rate of 186,000 miles a second, consumes more than three years in passing from it

to us. Sirius is more than sixteen years distant,
Arcturus more than twenty-four years, and our
Pole star more than forty years. And so on into
hundreds and thousands of years. There are stars
whose light has been spurring toward us on a
straight line ever since the creation of man and
has not yet reached us. Nay, there are among the
stars visible in our larger telescopes some which
if annihilated just now would continue to appear
in our sky for millions of years.

So we see that our Solar Family is spaced off
from every other after a wonderful manner. And
this probably correctly represents the average
abyss between the Solar Families. What an
amazing abyss it is! The stars are fond of society,
as we shall see further on, but they do not like to
come into very close quarters with one another—
do not like to be embraced and kissed on both
cheeks by their neighbors. Their mutual regards
are on the *Keep your distance* principle.

We have heard of a city of magnificent distances.
This seems absurd to us—to us who have seen on
what scale the heavens are built. How the mighty
spaces swallow up all our petty earthly units of
dimension: and even those in use between the
members of our Solar Family! The people who
hurry about the earth in our day and get quite a

name as travelers, seem mere snails or fixtures as we think of the travel implied in journeying to the nearest fixed star. A family sets itself down on one of our western prairies, and complains that it finds itself fifty miles from a neighbor. Preposterous! What if it should find itself 360,000 million times that distance from the nearest house! Then it might well call itself a hermit, and feel cut off from society. Ye who scamper round the world in ninety days and make nothing of it, what say you to an outing and a scamper at the same brisk pace to *Alpha Centauri?* It will only take you 180 millions of years, and what are they to an immortality, or to one whose business it is to kill time!

That solitary western settler is able to console himself in his solitude with the idea that it will probably be very short-lived, and that even to-morrow may see the fifty miles of his isolation dwindled to as many rods. But no Solar Family can have such a consolation as it strains its gaze across the enormous sky-prairie to where dwells its nearest neighbor. It will never see that nearest star one bit nearer. Perhaps it does not want to. Perhaps it sees that any closer neighborhood might be troublesome. Proximities in the heavens, as well as on the earth, threaten complications.

It takes no little care in our crowded human society to get along without embarrassments and entanglements. And, doubtless, the Solar Families cannot afford to get very near to one another. Distance is the condition of safety. They must not come to close quarters. They must give one another a wide berth. Else something dreadful would happen. If we should find even pleasant-faced Arcturus with his fleet of worlds approaching us under full sail, and year by year swelling on our sight till as large as the sun and larger, we should be alarmed and have reason to be. An indignation meeting of all the planets would be held; the Sun presiding. They would pass resolutions of the strongest kind against immigration, and then with one consent would rush to repel the immigrant and would destroy themselves in destroying him.

When we think of the almost immeasurable intervals between the Solar Families do we get the impression of an awful loneliness for each—as we do when we see an island parted from other lands by vast stretches of stormy ocean? Let us dismiss the impression. We are not entitled to it. Who knows that the luminous islands above are so many shut-in societies—are so many everlasting quarantine grounds? No one. The islands of this world are musical with the plash and dash of oceans over which come and go the white fleets of commerce and empire, and under which pass the electric cables of constant intercourse with all lands—may it not be so with the shining archipelagos of the greater deep above us? May not they be musically lapped by an ocean of ether filling all the stellar spaces; and may not a vast system of inter-communication be actively in play between the orbs lying so immensely apart? It is true that we hear nothing of the plash and dash of those almost spiritual waves—see nothing of etherial fleets going and coming over submerged highways of thought and speech on which the lightning runs express from star to star. And yet in that vast Polynesia above us not a single island but is in close sympathy and intercourse with all its sister islands. Gravitations innumerable web together the most distant stars. Light is a magnificent and everlasting go-between; and its trains come and go at all hours of the day and night. Light is the universal language among the Solar Families. Between star and star, photographs are being exchanged every moment. The latest events in each are being telegraphed on sunbeams to every other. And it would not be so very strange if some one should by and by discover that the stellar spaces are traversed by great gulf-streams of energy more swift and potential than even light and gravity. And, let us not forget the holy angels, those mighty travelers who minister to the heirs of salvation.

How distances on the earth dwindle to growing children? How they have dwindled to all within the memory of men now living, as ease and speed of inter-communication have improved! Is it too much to hope that the time will come to the good man when his immortal wings will easily bridge in a moment even such mighty chasms as part star from star! Nay, O soul, thou canst spin a suspension bridge, as the spider does, out of *thyself* (out of thine own holy thoughts, feelings, purposes, character) and thou shalt anchor one end of it on this world and God will anchor the other end on the other side of the abyss and then thou shalt travel over it some day from star to star—nor need a small eternity in which to do it.

# IX.

# OTHER SOLAR FAMILIES—II.

SIZE.

UNITIES.

# OTHER SOLAR FAMILIES—II.

How do other Solar Families compare with our own as to size and importance? Our own is no dwarf. Our own is not wanting in grandeur. Eight great worlds accompanied by twenty moons, hundreds of asteroids, and millions of comets wheel mightily through a home and astrodrome whose breadth is more than 5,400 millions of miles. Is this a fair specimen of the Solar Families? Are some of them far grander than this?

If we could only bring actual vision to bear on the planets and other dependent bodies belonging to some of those far-off celestial households! But this no astronomer has yet done, or is in immediate danger of doing. It is a "far cry" even to *Alpha Centauri*. And yet it is by no means incredible that another generation of astronomers may do the feat that is now impossible to us.

For the present—at least until we "shuffle off the mortal coil" that now prevents us from un-

folding our wings, having the freedom of the
stellar spaces, and personally visiting the remoter
heavens—we must try to find some reasonable
substitute for sight.   Is there any such substitute?
Have we any means of knowing how large and
grand any of the distant Solar Families are?

Some weight should be given to the current impression among astronomers.  This is that many
of the remote planetary systems represented to us
by the fixed stars are far grander than our own
system; and that these grander systems belong to
stars which are far grander than our sun.   Different people might give different reasons for this
impression.  Some, perhaps, would give no reason
at all—saying that with them it is a matter of *feeling* rather than of argument.  Do I laugh at
them?  Do I call them unscientific?  By no means.
For a feeling is itself often of the nature of argument—being the forecast shadows of many arguments on the way; being the impression made on
us by truths not yet individualized but as it were
held in solution in the air.  We breathe the air;
we unconsciously absorb its logical contents; we
find ourselves disposed to believe things for which
as yet we can give no satisfactory reason.  So,
apart from reasons, we should allow a certain
weight to impressions that have become current

in the astronomical world—to the impression that in the distant heavens there are grander Solar Families than our own.

But cannot the reasons for this impression that lie latent in the astronomical air be brought out of hiding; or, as the chemists say, precipitated? Let us see. Suppose we have found a star larger than our sun. What reason have we for thinking that this star has a larger retinue of worlds than our sun has?

In the first place, it would accord with the analogy of our own satellite systems—in which, in general, the larger planets have the larger moon systems. Little Mercury has no moon at all; but the great frontier planets are the centres of great systems—especially those greatest planets of all, Jupiter and Saturn. What a glorious octave belts Saturn and makes music to our eyes if not to our ears! And yet still larger Jupiter has a still larger and more brilliant family if estimated by its total of sizes and weights. In these respects its five moons are more than equal to the eight moons of Saturn. Is it an unheard of thing for five men, or five principles, or five luminaries to outweigh and outshine double the number?

In the second place, it is one of the conditions of stability in our Solar Systems, as La Place has

9

shown, that the mass of its sun be very large in comparison with the total of all the other masses in the system. As a matter of fact it contains about eight hundred times as much matter as all the planets put together. This seems to mean that a solar system may safely be made large in proportion to the largeness of the central orb; and that so there would be a waste of construction and power in a system whose size is not proportioned to the size of the central body. But such waste is contrary to the observed habit of Nature. She is a great economist. Like the Master who made her, she "gathers up the fragments that nothing be lost."

But the main consideration remains to be stated. It is that, so far as we can see, the main purpose of a sun is to furnish light and heat and government to surrounding worlds. Hence the larger the stores of these things provided by its Maker in any system the larger that system may be presumed to be. Otherwise there would be waste. God would not provide a furnace out of proportion to the work to be done—what wise person would!

When we find the commissariat of a wise general to be large we conclude that his army is large. When we find that the coinage of a well-governed country is immense we infer that an

immense business calls for it. When "a hundred lights are glancing in yonder mansion fair,"
and we find the tables laid with hundreds of
covers we think we may safely infer that a great
gathering is expected. So if we should find
among the fixed stars a sun that equals a hundred such suns as ours in lighting, heating, and
governing power we think we can safely infer a
correspondingly great sphere of influence. The
greater admiral should have in charge the greater
celestial fleet. The wider celestial empire befits
the greater monarch.

It seems, then, that we may learn how a distant
Solar Family compares with our own in size and
importance whenever we can learn how its sun
compares with ours in brightness. This can be
done in some twenty cases—the cases of stars
whose distances from us have been found. The
distance of a star being known, we ask ourselves
how much less light and heat would our sun give
us if removed from us as far as the star is. This
question is easily answered by the law that the
intensity of a radiant force at any point varies
inversely as the square of the distance of the
radiant body from that point. That is, if our sun
were carried away to twice its present distance,
its light and heat to us would be only a quarter of

what it now is. If removed 200,000 times its present distance it would mean 40,000 millions times less to us as a luminary than it does now. But we have delicate instruments called photometers which can compare the light of our sun with that of a star; and we find that *Alpha Centauri* is about twice as brilliant as our sun would be at the same distance; *Sirias* 63 times more brilliant; *Polaris* 86 times; *Capella* 430 times; Arcturus 516 times; Alcyone 12,000 times. That is, Alcyone is equivalent as a luminary to 12,000 such suns as ours.

This is not exactly the same thing as saying that Alcyone is 12,000 times *larger* than our sun: for it is conceivable that suns of the same size may differ in the intensity of their light and heat, as well as in their quantity of matter. But probably in an average of stars the size will be in proportion to the amount of light emitted.

So we see that some of the Solar Families are vastly grander than that to which we belong. Our own celestial household is no trifle—as we would be apt to realize if compelled to put a girdle about some of its members, or to stretch a surveyor's chain, unit by unit, along the orbits through which they move. But how much grander must be a household whose chief is 12,000 suns strong! That must be one of the very sublimest of physical things—whether we consider the number of its orbs, or their size, or the immensity of the spaces which they dominate. And yet none can venture to say that even this sublimest Solar System we have up to the present happened to discover is the sublimest that exists. Among the millions of stellar families yet to be explored by us, living or dead, doubtless there are some far more colossal and grand than that which hides behind the glories of the great Pleiad.

But even now Merope hangs her head and drops her veil. When we look at our Solar System quite by itself, and measure it by standards current on the earth, it seems a mighty object; and we find ourselves disposed to receive congratulations on the size of the house we live in, of the farm we cultivate, of the country to which we belong. But a larger knowledge punctures our pride. As soon as our balloon soars high enough to get a full view of some of our neighbors it is completely riddled by their greater glories. It collapses. What went up as a rocket comes down like the stick. Poor, outshone sister Merope is weeping behind her veil.

But humility is useful though tearful.

Those distant Solar Families, more than a hundred millions in number, removed from us by such wonderful abysses, and, many of them, far grander than our own—what further do we know about them? Very little; if we insist on using the word knowledge in its strictest sense. Very much; if we are not unreasonable and will accept such evidence as governs us in our most important daily affairs.

1.  *They are all material.*

The abyss between them and us is one of space and not of nature. They are made up of the same general sort of substance that we see under our feet and closely around us. It is not an easy idea for some—but they might have been substance without being matter. But they are not. The spectra of the stars show that they are all incandescent matter; and if the purpose of a star is to light and warm attendant worlds, these worlds themselves must be material; for only matter can be warmed and lighted by matter.

2.  The distant Solar Families are not only material, but are, to some extent at least, composed of the same sorts of matter we find in our own world.

The matter directly about us is of many very different sorts—as hydrogen, nitrogen, iron, and so on. Now it is conceivable that these earthly sorts of matter are only a small part of the varieties that actually exist. In the vast round of wealthy Nature there may be materials differing as widely from all such elements known to us as iron does from hydrogen; and the distant Solar Families might have been made up exclusively of such strange elements. But, as a matter of fact, they are not. *Might have been* is a very poor guide as to what actually is. Our spectroscopes tell us that hydrogen, sodium, magnesium, and iron are present in almost all the stars; and that no star whose spectrum has been examined has failed to show the presence of one or more familiar earthy substances.

This establishes the close kinship of the *stars* with our earth. But how do we know that the invisible planets that wait on any given star partake of this kinship? We cannot answer; with the evolutionist that planets are the children of stars and would naturally be like their parents—that planets were centrifugally drawn out of stars and therefore must be, to some extent, composed of the same elements. We can only say that it is very unlikely that earthly sorts of matter should exist in all the visible celestial worlds in all parts of the heavens and not exist in the invisible worlds in close connection with these—especially in view of the fact already noticed that our sun and the earth have some elements in common. Would it not be uncommonly rough on both analogy and induction to think otherwise? Have we not a right to presume that the almost measureless abyss that parts us from the distant Solar Families is yet spanned by a bridge of cosmical consanguinity. The heavens and the earth are blood relations, though their lots are cast so far apart.

3. The distant Solar Families are largely subject to the same forces and laws and phenomena that are found in our own system.

The stars, like our sun, are worlds intensely on fire. They pour forth in every direction, among the planets that surround them, floods of light and heat. This light and heat in which the planets are bathed and through which they are constantly swimming, are everywhere demonstrably the same—obeying the same laws of radiation, refraction, reflection, and diffusion which are noticed in the earth. So far as these great elements are concerned, the elements which affect us so powerfully in a thousand different ways, the situation of all the stellar systems is precisely the same.

So much for their environment. Now consider again the similarity of materials composing all these stellar systems. All of them matter. All of them matter of the same sorts as our own—at least to some extent, and perhaps wholly. Are we not bound to think, in the absence of all evidence to the contrary, that this general sameness of constitution carries with it the same forces and laws? Will not the same substance behave in very much the same way wherever located, especially under the same harness of environment? *Mutant cælum, sed non animum.*

For example. Gravity, and a particular law of gravity, belong to every sort of matter found in our Solar Family. Whether it is oxygen, or carbon, or a metal, or some as yet unrecognized element, makes no difference; it attracts other matter in every direction, and attracts with a force proportioned directly to its quantity of matter and inversely to the square of the distance between itself and the attracted body. This behavior is found by ample astronomical experience to be altogether independent, within our own broad system, of the sort of matter and of locality. Neptune swims through his frontier orbit in obedience to precisely the same principle and law that govern Mercury. Remove Neptune to the distance of

Sirius or Polaris and it would, doubtless, behave in the same way. Matter does not leave its own nature behind when it sets off on its travels—as some Christians are maliciously said to do—but carries away with itself every natural attribute, whether the travel be to the other side of the world or to the other side of creation.

We therefore conclude that the matter, of whatever sorts it may be, which makes up the distant Solar Families, attracts in every direction, and according to the law that rules everywhere in our system. What follows? It follows that their planets are globes; for the globular shape is the goal which all other shapes would sooner or later reach under the influence of gravity—not only where the mass is vaporous or fused, but even when in a rigid state. It also follows, as Newton has shown mathematically, that these globes in any system that does not at once perish, must revolve about their primaries in obedience to what are known as Kepler's Laws: that is, must revolve in circles or ellipses, must revolve so as to make lines joining them to their primaries describe equal areas in equal times, must revolve so that the squares of their periodic times shall be as the cubes of their mean distances from their primaries. Whenever, therefore, we look away to the more than one hundred millions of fixed stars that shine about the very threshold of creation we are to conceive of them as so many centres of revolution to huge globes that go and come in swift, silent, harmonious, and calculable movements that are quite like those we admire in our own system. Each star is the centre of a vast hippodrome where worlds are the mettlesome steeds. These orbed coursers run their mighty rounds with almost incredible swiftness and yet never weary, never stumble, never swerve, never collide. And why? A harness that never gives way is on every one of them. A yoke that never breaks presses every thunder-clad neck. And both harness and yoke are everywhere of the same pattern—the pattern of our terrestrial gravity that makes the apple fall and holds Neptune to his sphere. And the charioteer is—*not* Phæton. The Father drives his own chariot. And this is why the heavens are not ablaze to-day.

# X.

# OTHER SOLAR FAMILIES—III.

## OTHER UNITIES.

# OTHER SOLAR FAMILIES—III.

In stating what we know of the far-away Solar Families that gather about the fixed stars, I have said that they are material systems; that they are systems, to some extent at least, composed of the same sorts of matter found in our world; that they are systems largely subject to the same forces and laws and phenomena that appear in our own system.

To these three points of likeness to our system let us now add a fourth:

4. The distant Solar Families are in general *stable systems.* They continue unimpaired from age to age.

Our own system with its complicate movements and inter-actions (sometimes called disturbances) has stood the wear and tear of uncounted millenniums of historic and geologic time. For aught I know, and for aught anyone knows, it is in as sound a condition to-day as it ever was. More than this—as we have seen, it has been mathematically established that this system which has actually defied the ages so long contains in itself no element of instability; but, unless acted upon destructively from without, will continue as it is forever.

Have the distant Solar Families a like steadfastness? The answer which the heavens send back to this question is clearly an affirmative. In general the stars which represent these remote systems shine on without material change from age to age. They stand fast forever. Like the sun and moon, they "endure throughout all generations." The ancient constellations look down upon us still. The ship Argo is still plowing the celestial deeps, Cassiopeia is still sitting on her throne, Hercules is still holding aloft his giant club, and not one sparkling jewel has disappeared from the belted and sworded form of great Orion. Rainy Hyades, sweet Pleiades, Mazzaroth in his season, Arcturus and his sons, are all shining on us as they shone on Kepler, on Hipparchus, on Job, and doubtless on Adam. The Berlin star-maps that give us so faithfully the aspects of the heavens to-day are, no doubt, a faithful picture in general of the heavens as they appeared 5,000 years ago, or of the heavens as they will appear 5,000 years hence.

There are certain noticeable changes among the
stars, as we must soon see; but, with a few seeming exceptions, they are such as need imply no
catastrophe to the systems where they occur.

This permanence in the stars means permanence
in the systems of which they are the centres.
Primary and satellites are fast bound up together.
They are the hub, spokes, and rim of one wheel
around which passes a strong and closely fittting
tire of steel. The interlacings of natural law are
such that when one member suffers all the members suffer with it. Ruptures, dislocations, derange-
ments of all sorts, even in the extremities of the
body, report themselves at once to the heart for
sympathy. The breaking up of a family does not
leave its head unharmed: A ruined kingdom is a
king in ruins. So a ruined stellar system would
at once proclaim itself in its sun. Orbits broken
up, planet colliding with planet or impinging
on its sun, would cause great conflagrations and
make that sun to blaze out into vast and unwonted
brightness—a phenomenon never known in the
case of the great majority of stars.

The great majority of the distant Solar Families
are, therefore, like our own in the matter of stability. Our own system, though its members are
always wrestling with one another; always rush-

10

ing hither and thither in steeple-chase fashion and apparently at random; always straining to fly off in a tangent from the head of the family; yet somehow manage never to come to grief, and are found under mighty domestic bonds never to come to it in any of their endless circumnavigations. Similarly stable appear most of those remoter Solar Families represented to us by the Solar stars. They have immense faculty for lasting. They have no faculty at all for committing suicide. So they endure indefinitely. And it is a pleasant thing to some of us, amid the frailties and decays and vanishings of so many things about us, not excepting our human households and our bodily selves, to look away to the eternal stars and see mirrored in their unfading eyes, not only celestial households that are never broken up but also the unchangeableness of Him who is from everlasting to everlasting.

But here we are obliged to say that, although in general stable systems,

5. The distant Solar Families are sometimes the scene of vast disturbances and changes—in this respect, too, like our own system.

The mighty forces pent up in the bosom of the earth have often, within historic time, broken loose in great convulsions. Before man appeared, still greater cataclysms took place and left their records in disrupted strata, upheaved mountains, buried forests, and extinguished animal races. Some go so far as to say that the earth was once wholly vaporous, or at least molten—inferring it partly from the shape of the earth, which is that which a fluid would take if revolving as at present under the action of gravity. But, inasmuch as this shape is also that which even a rigid cube would finally take under the same circumstances in the course of unlimited time, this inference is hardly warranted. There is, however, no uncertainty about the fact that the time will come when the "elements will melt with fervent heat and the earth and the works that are therein shall be burned up."

This great event, unless some shielding miracle is interposed, will be great to our neighbors as well as greatly disastrous to ourselves. When a house is wrapped in flames how shall near neighbors escape a scorching? But even now we see in our neighbor-planets, and especially in the tremendously scarred and shattered surface of the moon, signs of terrible upheaval and convulsions —such as give life-color to the theory that anciently a large planet, swinging between Mars and Jupiter, burst into hundreds of fragments that now appear as the asteroids.

"When in heaven the stars about the glittering moon beam loveliest in the breathless air, and in clear outline appear every hill, sharp peak, and woody dell; deep upon deep the sky breaks open and each star shines forth while joy fills the shepherd's heart." When, on some fair night like this which Homer sang, we look around on the earth so quietly sleeping under her spangled curtains— look up on moon and planets looking down on the slumberer so softly and peacefully, it seems as if it had never been, and never could be, otherwise— all things steeped in eternal calm! Nevertheless this peaceful system of ours has seen rough times. It has come to its crown in the usual way—through crosses. It has not navigated the celestial deeps these thousands of years without encountering some foul weather, and getting some heavy strains. It must have been extremely well put together or it would have been a wreck long ago. If it could tell in fitting human speech all it has gone through it would beat all the romancers, and, perhaps, all the necromancers.

Over against this set the following instances of stars suddenly appearing where none had ever been noticed; sometimes brighter than stars of the first magnitude; remaining thus for a short time, and then gradually fading away. The first instance on record was observed by Hipparchus, 134 B. C. In 380 A. D. a star blazed forth near *Alpha Aquilæ* which shone for three weeks as splendidly as Venus, then disappeared, and has never since been seen. In 1572 a new star suddenly appeared in Cassiopea: when first noticed it was as bright as Sirius, and finally could be seen at midday: in about a month it began to fade, and in sixteen months had entirely disappeared. Other like cases occurred in 1604, 1848, and 1866.

Now we cannot suppose that these are cases of stars newly created and almost immediately extinguished ; nor cases of old stars suddenly transferred astounding distances toward us, and then almost as suddenly taken back on our visual line to their old sites—as if a mistake had been made and mended. God does not take back his work in this way. Nor is it credible that the facts can be due to the sudden removal and as sudden return of some very great interposing opaque body that never removes again. The only satis- • factory explanation seems to be that certain old stars suddenly received a vast increase of light, either from temporary conflagration of some planets in their neighborhood, or from the falling into themselves of some planet, or great meteoric swarms like that through which we plow our

luminous way in November. In either case a
mighty disturbance is involved. A planet breaking into universal flame is a catastrophe. A sun
absorbing into itself material for a hundredfold
light and heat would act tremendously on its
whole retinue of worlds, and especially on its near
neighbors. What would be the effect in our
system if, from any cause, our sun should suddenly
take on a hundredfold brightness? A miracle
would be needed for the preservation of at least
every near planet. Alas, for Mercury—unless
something broader and diviner than the ægis of immortal Jove could be interposed. Well, perhaps
that diviner shield *was* interposed in the cases mentioned, as we hope will be done for Venus and
Mars (to say nothing of the Moon) in the day
when the earth for a short time will become a sun.

Even strictly logical inferences are a poor substitute for sight and the other senses. Not poor
as a basis for information ; for nine-tenths of our
science and practical wisdom stands on nothing
better ; but poor as a means of conviction and
vivid impression. The reader of the account I am
now giving of the Solar Families in the distant
heavens may only imperfectly grasp the argument ; or, grasping it, soon find the conclusions
growing dim in the memory. But if he could do

what a certain French astronomer has lately pre-
tended to do—could actually get rid of gravity
and certain other corporeal drawbacks, and take
to himself levity and certain other supernatural
aids, and go voyaging among those remote systems, and examine on the spot their various features with all his five senses, doubtless the result
would be far more satisfactory. The facts would
be vastly more vivid as well as more abundant;
and would never fade from his thought so long as
thought itself should remain. And how long is
that?

But, alas, for the present we are helplessly tied
down to earth. We must content ourselves without flying and having the freedom of all the
spaces. The best we can do is to use our senses
as far as they will go and then supplement by
inductions and deductions and analogies and, at a
pinch, by the "scientific imagination" of our time,
stiffened somewhat by Locke and Bacon, to say
nothing of Aristotle. Trying to do this, we have
in former chapters reached certain conclusions as
to those remote stellar families for which the
fixed stars stand—viz., they are made of that particular substance which we call matter; they are,
to some extent at least, composed of the same
sorts of matter we find on the earth; they largely

present the same forces, laws, and phenomena that appear in our own system ; they are in general stable systems, though they have been in some cases the theatres of vast disturbance and change. To these five points of likeness to our own system, let us now add another.

6.   The distant Solar Families are all in course of translatory motion—as is our own system.

Our entire system is not only in motion about its own centre of gravity, but this centre is itself ever being transferred to distant regions. By no possibility can any celestial body always remain in the same district of space. The great law of universal attraction forbids. Were our sun once brought to absolute rest and then left to itself it would at once begin to move again under the stress of an attracting universe—unless it chanced to be already at that point in the universe where all its attractions are in equilibrium. In modern times nobody supposes that our earth, or even our sun, is the center of the creation.

In fact we find that our sun, besides moving about the common centre of gravity of its system, is moving away toward the distant heavens, carrying with itself of course all the members of its family. Some human families disintegrate easily: the Solar Family disintegrates never. A few human families stick together under all circumstances : the Solar Family does the same, and each member says to every other, " Whither thou goest I will go, and where thou lodgest I will lodge, and where thou diest I will die, and there will I be buried ; naught but death shall part thee and me."

The stars in the constellation Hercules are observed to be separating more and more from year to year, while the stars in the opposite quarter are gradually drawing together. This is just what would happen if our sun with all its planet-dom were in motion toward Hercules. Besides, the spectra of the stars in this constellation show that they are all approaching us. By carefully noting the rate of this approach astronomers feel able to say that we are crossing the heavens at the rate of 150,000,000 miles a year. This motion for the present seems to be in a straight line ; indeed the line we have been moving on for nearly a hundred years does not differ sensibly from a straight line. But we know that it must really be a curve. To prevent collisions and wreckage it is as necessary that suns and systems move in orbits about centres of gravity as that individual planets should do so. The reason that our motion seems rectilinear is the exceeding largeness of the orbit we are traversing. Ah, how wonderfully large that orbit must be whose arc of nearly fifteen billions of miles hardly deserts a tangent through its whole length! If our lives, year after year, were keeping as close to a certain straight line as is the path of the sun we should have considerably more reason to congratulate ourselves than we now have.

Truly, our system as it rushes through space has a far away look in its eyes! It means a mighty voyage. Maedler thought it meant putting a girdle about Alcyone. If so, it will take some millions of years to accomplish its purpose; for Alcyone is some 300,000 Neptunian sun-distances from us.

Now the translatory motion which we observe in our own system, and which we know must exist in all the distant Solar Families, has been actually noticed in a great many of them. Careful watching shows that the "fixed" stars are by no means fixed, but are slowly creeping about in all directions; and, in the case of many stars, these motions have been measured. Their annual amounts are very small—practically zero as compared with those of the planets; requiring for their detection exact instruments and careful watching, and not noticeably changing to the naked eye the positions of the stars relative to one another from age to age. But "many a little makes a mickle" in the heavens as well as on the earth ; and, after thousands of years from now, the configuration of constellations will be found to have sensibly changed. Striking charts have been made, showing the difference between *Ursa Major* as it now is and as it will appear 36,000 years hence—i. e., if all things go on for that great time as they are now doing. But who can vouch for that?

These minute motions of the stars, which, however in long periods accumulate into great changes of place, are due partly to our own motion through space, and partly to the motion of the stars themselves. Knowing the amount and direction of our own motion, we can subtract its effect from the total apparent motion of any given star. We find a remainder and are able to measure it. This is called the star's proper motion. Whether this motion is toward us or away from us can be determined by the spectroscope—as can also the amount of the approach or recession.

All these proper motions, like the translatory motion of our sun, are apparently rectilinear. But they must really be in orbits. They appear otherwise because the orbits are so vast that the curves described within our observation do not differ sensibly from straight lines. Our sun, with his body-guard of planets about him, is going a great round at a great pace ; but he has for companions in this at least a hundred millions of other families. It is a trackless void through which they are moving ; but not one of them is journeying blindly or uncertainly. He knows just where he is going and just how much time he has to spend in his journey ; and he will go as surely, and as certainly come round on time, as if underlaid by steel tramways.

We say "come round." But we can say more than this demonstrable thing. It is that other equally demonstrable thing that all the other Solar Families are rounding about the same centre of gravity that governs and pivots us. Among the more than one hundred millions of such families belonging to our cosmical archipelago there must be many different secondary centres of revolution ; but this we are sure of that there must be one final centre about which all the revolutions are curved. If it is not in the Pleiades, as Maedler inferred from certain star driftings, it is *somewhere* within our cosmical district. Can we do better than shake hands with our illustrious astronomer who has done so much for stellar science, and be thankful that he has felt able to suggest to us such a magnificent metropolis for such magnificent navies to make such magnificent circumnavigations about ?

Wherever this common centre may be, we must remember that, from the necessity of the case, unless it is the gravity-centre of the whole material universe, it must be itself in motion. Hence the majestic rounds of which I have written, cannot be curves returning into themselves, as circles or ellipses, but rather abortive attempts at such curves, resulting in endless spirals that are always seeking new regions in which to uncoil themselves. So none of the countless Solar Families ever revisits a spot where it has once been.

Always moving day with it ? Yes. Always on the road, bag and baggage ? Yes, and more. For it is not only always emigrating, but it is always emigrating to a wholly new and unknown country. And it will never be otherwise. However far the Solar Families may travel they will never find spots exactly to their mind, where they can settle down, set up their household gods, and say, *This is home*. Well, this looks a little unpleasant to some of us who dislike the nomadic sort of life ; but there are some people who are born travelers, and who are never so much at home as when

away from home.  To such people, including all
the Solar Families, the words of the prophets will
not be as pathetic as they are to me:  "Weep
sore for him that goeth away ; for he shall return
no more, nor see his native country."

# XI.

## OTHER SOLAR FAMILIES IV.

### UNANSWERED QUESTIONS.

## XI.

# OTHER SOLAR FAMILIES—IV.

UNANSWERED QUESTIONS.

There are very many unanswered questions in all the sciences. Of course questions are always in order; it is necessary to ask them, and necessary to try to give satisfactory answers; otherwise there can be no progress. But it is one thing to *try* to answer a question and quite another thing to really answer it. Attempted explanations do not always explain—not even when made by scientific men. Even astronomers sometimes confessedly fail. See some examples in connection with the distant Solar Families which we have been considering.

1. What is the explanation of what are called variable stars?

Very many stars shine with a variable lustre. In not a few cases the change is extremely irregular—following no conceivable law. In other cases the change is periodical—the stars gradually fading from a maximum to a certain point and then

gradually returning to their original lustre, which
they retain for a while and then begin to repeat
the process. The periods are of all sizes from a
few hours to a few centuries. Among the short
periods the most remarkable, perhaps, is that of
*Algol* which generally appears as a star of the
second magnitude and continues thus for 61 hours;
it then fades and in less than 4 hours becomes of
the fourth magnitude, and thus remains about
twenty minutes; it then increases and in 4 hours
regains its greatest lustre. The whole circle of
change is complete in less than three days.

To what are these changes of aspect owing?

Of course a change in the apparent lustre of a
star would be made by a change in its distance
from us; also by a special accumulation of sun-
spots on one side of it if rotating;—also by the
passing of opaque bodies, luminous or non-luminous, between us and the star. Some cases of
variation can be explained tolerably well by one
or more of these suggestions; others can hardly
be covered by all of them when patched together
into a coat of many colors; and there are others
still whose nakedness cannot be half covered by
such a patch-work garment however deftly put
together. So astronomers are wont to confess.
Says Lockyer, "The cause of the change of bright-

ness in variable stars is one of the most puzzling questions in the whole domain of Astronomy."

2. Unanswered questions as to the various colors of the stars and consequently of the Solar Families belonging to them.

Close examination, especially in tropical regions, shows large differences as to color among the stars. In fact all the colors of the rainbow are found among them. Most of them, like our sun are white: but Aldebaran, Antares, and Betelguese are red; Capella, Rigel, and Procyon are blue; Sirius, Vega, and Altair are green; Arcturus is yellow. One group of a hundred stars resembles a bouquet of fancy jewelry, where the ruby, and emerald and amethyst and pearl and sapphire and diamond blend their glories.

These different colors must be due to the stars themselves, and the effect must be to give to the surrounding planets as many differently colored days. How a red day, or a green, or a blue must affect the appearance of a planet we căn judge from the hues sometimes cast over our landscapes at sunset and sunrise and at other times when the air is heavy with vapors, or from the rich colors that bathe the interior of some sanctuary as the light streams in through its painted windows.

If we ask whether these variously colored days that flood the distant Solar Families do not naturally suggest the many sidedness of the Divine power and skill, and also suggest properly that He who loves variety in the hues of earthly gems and flowers also loves such variety among those celestial gems and flowers that we call the stars, some of us will not puzzle long for an answer. But what if we ask such questions as the following? Do days of different colors mean different chemical and physiological, as well as pictorial, effects on animal and vegetable life, and if so what? Do they mean different stages of conflagration in the stars, different ages for the stars and for their surrounding worlds? Do they mean different constituent elements in the stars, or at least in their gaseous envelopes? In the case of a blue star, does the blueness mean that there are none but blue rays in the light of the star, or that all but the blue rays have been sifted out by encompassing gases? Such questions have never been satisfactorily answered. We put them on file for the use of—perhaps another generation. The prospect of *our* solving them is bluer than any star.

But it seems that the color of a star, though generally steadfast, does sometimes change in the course of long periods. Sirius, now green, was once described as fiery red, then as white. Capella, now pale blue, was once red and afterwards yellow. In general these changes are very slow; but they have been known to be very rapid—as in the case of a star observed by *Tycho Brahe in 1572*, which changed from white to red and then to yellow and then back again to white, all in 16 months. What is the cause of these changes? Astronomers have to confess ignorance. About all they can say is that such changes imply "incessant movement and transformation going on in the remote heavens;" but as to what and how great these movements and transformations are, we still need light. Hypotheses, of course, are not wanting: but on none of them have we been able to sail far on our Congo toward the dark interior before being compelled by cataracts to disembark.

3. Any recent creations among the distant Solar Families?

That there was a time when not one of these systems existed is plain from the Scriptures. But it is conceivable that, since that time, there has been a succession of world-creations—star after star springing into being at intervals at as many successive fiats of the Almighty. This successive-ness is not only conceivable, but even seems more likely to be actual, than that God should have brought the whole visible cosmos into being at one stroke of his will and then forever ceased creating.

If star-creations have been successive, the question naturally arises, Have any such creations taken place in our time, or in the time of our astronomy? Stars have appeared where none had been noticed before, they have appeared suddenly, and, perhaps in a few cases, they have remained undimmed permanently. Now these stars *may* be new creations: but they also *may* be old stars situated just beyond the frontier of vision which, suddenly receiving a vast access of fuel, flash up into visibility and so continue for hundreds of years. So we cannot decide. Our science as yet can neither affirm nor deny the creation of suns and systems within the historic time.

4. Any recent annihilations among the distant Solar Families?

It is commonly said that matter is never annihilated—it only changes its form and relations. It is true that no agency of man, and no natural process, either does or can make a single particle of matter cease to be. But what man and Nature cannot do God can. He can both make something out of nothing and reduce something to

nothing again.  He has done the one thing in
"creating the heavens and the earth"—in giving
existence to countless stellar systems in space once
absolutely vacant of matter.  He can do the other
thing—can at any moment reduce to absolute
vacancy any one of the great systems His will has
brought into being.  To-day Sirius with its pomp
of attendant globes is shining and wheeling in
almost infinite glory and dynamics: to-morrow,
let the Eternal will it, that wonderful astrodrome
shall be as empty of everything as it was before
the morning stars sang together.  This is what
God *can* do.  Has He ever done the like within
the time of our astronomy?

It is certainly conceivable that occasion may
have arisen for doing it.  As fitting occasion has
arisen for creating, so fitting occasion may have
come for absolutely destroying a Solar Family.
It has filled out its day, it has served its purpose,
it has fulfilled its mission, and why should it be
continued?  Perhaps it has become so saturated
with effete and corrupt elements and associations
that a clean riddance of the whole thing is the
pleasantest possible thought to a perfect being.
As we sometimes like to come as near as we can
to destroying a worn-out garment that has become
incurably ragged and unclean; as the authorities
of a town sometimes replace the primitive school

house which has become unsuited to the educational needs of the people by a larger and more commodious building; as a prosperous man replaces his original cabin with a finer dwelling to suit his better circumstances and larger needs; so God may do with a stellar system. We men cannot annihilate the old garment or buildings: the best thing we can do is to remove the materials to some out-of-the-way place, or turn them into flame and smoke and ashes: but, rather than be at the trouble of doing this, we would, if we could by merely willing it, annihilate the offensive materials just where they stand. It would be the simplest and most natural thing to do—for man or God.

But theory apart, what is the answer of facts to the question, Do the stars ever absolutely perish?

Some stars have disappeared from their places, and up to the present time have not reappeared. Sir Wm. Herschel mentioned 13 of this sort, and others have been noticed since.

Such are the facts. Do they show that some stars have gone into bankruptcy—ever paying out more than they receive and so at last becoming exhausted and insolvent? Of course the facts are perfectly consistent with the annihilation theory. But they are equally consistent with the idea that some of the lost stars were insensibly withdrawn from view by their own relative motion; that others were variables of long periods and will yet reappear; and that still others appear lost on account of the inaccurate observations and maps of all but recent times. If great Sirius, which has been known for ages as a non-variable, should suddenly disappear while we are looking at it and not appear again for many centuries, it might well be considered a perished star. But no such case has ever been known. All the cases of lost stars on record are cases in which inaccurate observation may be suspected, or which the theory of variable stars can explain.

It is not pleasant to confess ignorance. We would be glad to send an intelligent gaze into all depths and heights. "I do not know" is about the hardest confession that a young philosopher can make. So reluctant are some to make it that they are strongly tempted to christen questions and possibilities into science and proclaim them as such from the minarets of the world. This has often been done. But truths are not made by proclamation. Interrogation points cannot be proclaimed into periods, nor the subjunctive mood into the indicative. The interests of true science have often suffered sadly from premature decisions. They all have to be taken back. And, meanwhile, centuries have dragged a ball and chain because of the *ipse dixits* of some Aristotle or less.

# XII.

# SOLAR COMMUNITIES—I.

KNOTS.

HAMLETS.

TOWNS.

VILLAGES.

XII.

# SOLAR COMMUNITIES—I.

KNOTS—HAMLETS—TOWNS—VILLAGES.

Sometimes a family is solitary. It is located between towns—it is set down in the heart of a great western prairie. For miles and miles in every direction no other family can be found. The smoke that curls upward from its cabin never gets high enough to descry anywhere an answering column.

A few weeks pass. We take a second look at that lonely western family. Lo, it is no longer without neighbors. Two or three new cabins are within sight and easy reach of one another. We have a little neighborhood of families in close connection with one another but parted by great spaces from all similar neighborhoods. Another stage of settlement has been reached. Unity has become a small plurality. The hermit has become a hamlet. Smoke answers to smoke every morning, candle answers to candle every night. The light that beams from the window of one home beams into the window of another. If one family gets into trouble there is another at hand to give sympathy and help. Not only the pioneer but the van-guard of settlement has arrived. Listen! Is not the tramp of thousands behind them?

The Solar Families which we have thus far been considering have been solitaires, or what seemed to be such at first view. Each has seemed a single islet in a vast ocean otherwise unoccupied. Our own Solar Family is one of these lonely ones. It has no neighbor nearer than about 20,000 billions of miles: and a great many other celestial households are in the same hermit-like, secluded, quarantined condition. It is to be hoped that they are neither lazarettos, nor prisoners condemned to solitary confinement. I think they are not. There are quite too many of them. Some good families on the earth flourish best when well by themselves —why may it not be so among yonder families in the heavens?

But first impressions are sometimes misleading. It may be that some of these Solar Families that seem so lonely are not as lonely as they seem. Near neighbors draw together as we recede from them and at last appear as one. Some stars that seem hermits may really be knots and hamlets of stars. So let us look at them again carefully through our telescopes. Lo, a star which we had thought a unit divides up into two or three stars. We try that famous celibate Polaris and find him double. We try glorious Castor and Sirius and find that neither of them cares for single blessedness. We even find that *Gamma Andromedæ* is triple, *Epsilon Lyræ* quadruple; and that *Theta Orionis* is seven-fold. About 10,000 complex stars that shine as one to the naked eye have been discovered since the time of Sir Wm. Herschel. Doubtless many more will be found.

Now what do these facts mean? Not necessarily that the members composing a double or multiple star are closely together in space; for stars any distance apart would seem near if seen in nearly the same direction. But we are able to determine when the nearness is merely optical. If the component stars are found to have the same proper motion in direction and degree they must be physically connected and belong to the same local neighborhood. This condition is fulfilled in the case of by far the greater part of the double and multiple stars. The members of each are moving along the sky in company. The point toward which one is tending is that toward which all are tending. They keep step together like trained soldiers. This could not be unless they were bound up together as parts of the same physical system and were relatively near neighbors. But each of these neighbors must be regarded as the centre of a planetary system; and so each double or multiple star must mean a little neighborhood of as many Solar Families as there are components in the star. Thus in the case of the sextuple star *Sigma Orionis* we have six Solar Families forming a little commuity by themselves.

In some cases the component stars are nearly or quite equal; but generally there is considerable difference in size. Rigel, a splendid star in the left foot of giant Orion, is made up of one very large star and one very small. The same is true of Sirius. And we naturally suppose that there is a corresponding inequality in the size and importance of the planetary systems thus set together —one consisting, it may be, of a thousand worlds and another of ten. The unequal families which are apt to make up our human neighborhoods are projections on a small scale of facts in the sky.

By carefully watching the double and multiple stars, it has been found that in each of several hundreds of them there is not only a common proper motion of the component stars, but also that they are in course of REVOLUTION among themselves. One star revolves about another star; a pair of stars about another pair; a triplet about a triplet, and so on. How the eyes of Sir Wm. Herschel must have snapped when, on the night of Nov. 5, 1779, while comparing the position of the small companion of Castor with that set down twenty years before, he first caught the idea of this great fact—or rather, awoke to the fact that perhaps he had caught a sun in the act of revolving about a sun, a system of worlds revolving about a system—and how brightly his twin eyes must have shone on the shining twins above as he watched the slow unfolding of the orbit year by year till his peradventure was strengthened into a certainty and he could say in 1803, "Its period is about 342 years." There are few things that will so kindle the fires in a man's eye as the sense of having made a great discovery—perhaps because it will immortalize himself, and perhaps because it will benefit the world. It may be that the fire of both thoughts is in his heart and is flashing from his eyes.

Since that time the motions among the double stars have drawn much enthusiastic observation. About 13 of them have completed one or more revolutions: 28 have made more than half a revolution; 43 more than a quarter-revolution; and 156 have advanced more than twenty degrees on their orbits. Many others have traversed smaller

12

arcs, and yet arcs large enough to show the forms of the orbits, their inclinations to the line of sight, and their approximate periods. Most of these periods exceed a thousand years; but there are 22 stars whose periods are less than a century, and among them one hurries through its orbit after a hurricane fashion in 14 years.

Stars consisting of two members each, being the easiest to deal with, have naturally drawn the most attention from astronomers. But others have not been wholly neglected. The same process of revolution, though of a more complex pattern, has been noticted going on in multiple stars. Thus in the quadruple star *Epsilon Lyræ* whose stars appear in two pairs, it is found that the period of one pair is 1,000 years, of the other 2,000, and of both pairs about their common centre of gravity something short of a million of years. Each star in this system solves the difficult problem of compassing two shifting centres of attraction at the same time—a feat sometimes attempted by men, but rarely with success.

Generally, the orbits in connection with the double and multiple stars are extremely elliptical. In two cases, those of *Alpha Centauri* and *Gamma Virginis*, the orbits are nearly five times longer than they are broad, and generally the length exceeds the breadth by more than a quarter of itself. This is a hard nut for the friends of the nebular hypothesis to crack. Up to the present the only cracking heard has been that of the hammer.

In the cases where the distance of a double or multiple star is known, we can easily find the distance in miles between its members. And we find that the distance between the two stars which compose *61 Cygni* is considerably greater than that between Neptune and our Sun; though the interval between Sirius and its companion is less than that between Uranus and our Sun. And there are other double stars like Sirius in this respect. That is, there are systems of suns on a smaller scale than our system of planets.

In cases, too, where the distance of a double star is known we can weigh the stars—can find by Kepler's Third Law how the mass of matter in the component stars compares with that of our sun. Thus we find that the weight of Sirius is nearly 14 times that of our sun.

Of late we can do better than even this. For, by means of the spectroscope and photography, we can sometimes detect a double star when its duplicity is not visible in any telescope; also determine the distance between its members, the period of one about the other, and the sum of their masses in terms of our sun. This has been done, apparently, in the case of Mizar, the middle star in the tail of Ursa Major. This star has long been known as double, but it has lately been found by the spectroscope that the larger member is itself double, and that one of its members goes about the other in 104 days, and that the distance between the two is about the distance of Mars from our sun, and that their combined quantity of matter is nearly 40 times that of our sun. If now we could only measure the angular interval between these two components we could easily tell the distance of Mizar from us. The same process will enable us to verify the distances of some other stars as given by their parallaxes. Science always likes to reach the same result by independent processes. Assurance becomes doubly sure—if one knows what that means.

It is among the double and multiple stars that we find the most brilliant examples of colored suns. In *Iota Cancri* the larger member is orange, the smaller blue. In *Éta Cassiopeiæ* one member is white, the other a rich ruddy purple. In the triple star, *Gamma Andromedæ*, one member is orange-red, the other members are emerald green.

Of course this means for the Solar Family gathered about each star in these little Solar neighborhoods not only the light of several suns, but of several suns of different sizes and colors. These may be in the sky at the same time. Some may be rising while others are setting. Differently colored days or moons will sometimes succeed one another, and sometimes they will combine in a day or night tinted like a rainbow. There is room for infinite speculation as to the changes that would be needed in human beings to adapt them to such strange surroundings. Beyond all question the rational beings who, beyond all question, inhabit those distant worlds are fitted to their circumstances by Him who, beyond all question, made them. Men often make a misfit—God never. We may have reason to complain of our shoemaker or our tailor or our politician—some of the most grievous misfits of all lie at the door of the latter —perhaps he himself is a greater misfit than his work. But Omniscience never fails to adapt his creatures to their habitation—or rather their habitation to his creatures. As the Sabbath was made for man and not man for the Sabbath, so worlds were made for the sake of their inhabitants, and not inhabitants for the sake of the worlds—the palace for the king and not the king for the palace.

Besides homes somewhat loosely distributed, a township usually contains some in special proximity to one another—little neighborhoods so close that the homes composing them appear as one when viewed a little distance away. In some cases two or more families occupy the same dwelling. In all cases what one hears all are apt to hear; what one sees all are apt to see. The epidemic that attacks one may be expected to attack all; and when circumstances enhance the value of one homestead the others of course share in the advance. A fire well started in one will endanger all of them—so near to one another are they. It is a *knot* of families. They are cheek by jowl. Very possibly they are consanguineous. The father or grandfather built homes for his children by the side of his own. He wanted them all within easy reach. He wanted to be able to run in and out at any moment. So he nestled the dear ones snugly together about himself. These answer to the snugly compacted double and multiple stars.

But, besides some homes that are compacted into very close and small neighborhoods, a township often contains homes more sparsely distributed and which are separated from similar collections of homes in other towns by large spaces comparatively vacant of population. This also answers to what we see in the sky. Besides nucleated stars, that is stars knotted together by the naked eye, we see others in looser systems. In each of these systems the stars always appear separate, but they are in many cases relatively neighbors to one another in space and so must be physically connected together. Let us call such systems Solar Townships. Sir Wm. Herschell calls them groups.

A mere glance at the sky (and this, by the way, is all that most men give—greatly to their loss) shows us that the separate stars are not sown evenly through the vault, but that they often appear by twos and threes and still larger numbers. Sometimes the stars are so many and the intervals between them so small that we seem to see a celestial village: at other times the stars are so few and the intervals so large that we seem to see a celestial country-side whose homes are far from being within hailing distance of one another.

Doubtless some of these stellar neighborhoods are merely optical; the stars appear together, not because they are really neighbors in space, but because they happen to lie in nearly the same direction from us. But we have reason to believe that many of the groups are locally and physically connected. As men gather into families, families into hamlets, hamlets into towns, towns into states, states into empires, so the stars proceed in their grouping. First, the various satellites groups;

next, our planetary system forming a larger group inclusive of the others; next those close groups of suns represented by the double and multiple stars —all these minor groups lead us to expect still wider and more comprehensive groupings. So when we see a number of separate stars lying quite by themselves in the sky (many times more remote from other stars than they are from one another, like the Azores or Bahamas)—it is easy to believe that we have a continuation of past experience and see a celestial community bound up into one by special neighborly ties, though occupying a larger district and generally including a larger membership than any we have yet seen.

And here certain other circumstances come to our aid. We find that there is a certain family likeness among the stars of an apparent group— that their proper motions are the same, or have a certain suggestive reference to one another; that their spectra are alike and show that they are all approaching or receding from us at the same rate. Besides, has not the Calculus of Probabilities, confirmed by observation, shown that the greater part of the double and multiple stars are so many physical systems; and on like grounds must not the same be true of most of the apparent stellar groups? These adjutants help us greatly. These many littles make a mickle; and so astronomers are agreed that by far the larger part of apparent stellar groups imply so many local neighborhoods in each of which the members revolve about its centre of gravity.

The following things are true of these group systems. They consist of all numbers of stars, from two to hundreds. In each of three paws of *Ursa Major* is found a duad of stars, presumably a group—also five of its principal stars, many degrees apart, have a common proper motion and also a common motion in the line of sight; showing that they are a local neighborhood and so make a system by themselves. In Cassiopeia we find two triplets in each of which the stars are so near to one another, relatively to other stars, that we must regard them as belonging to the same system. Orion shows us still larger clans among the celestial highlands. And so we may ascend to groups whose members count up to scores and hundreds, and cover whole degrees of the vault. Some of these groups have in them stars whose distances from us have been measured, so that we know how far from us the groups are. Others contain no such stars, and we can only say of them that their remoteness is still more enormous, and that the intervals between members, separated sometimes by degrees instead of seconds, must also be enormous. The multiple stars give us knots of suns distributed somewhat on the scale of our planetary system : but in groups of stars the intervals are of quite another order of largeness. At most of the stars whose distances from us are known the entire orbit of Neptune subtends less than an angle of 2 '' : how far apart must be those still remoter stars whose intervals appear as several degrees! And yet we see that physically they belong together. Even when members of the same family are widely separated we can often see their relationship to one another without difficulty. Their family likeness betrays consanguinity though one is living in Boston, another in New York, and still another in Washington. "Is not your name X? I thought so. How much you resemble your two brothers!"

The form of the larger groups is irregular—as irregular as would be a line joining at any moment the outside planets of our own system. The stability of our own system shows that no particular conformation of a group is essential to its stability.

Among the larger groups are those known as the Pleiades, Hyades, and Præsepe. Of these the most famous is the Pleiades—appearing as six stars to the ordinary eye, seven or eight or even twelve to an extraordinary one, hundreds to the eye of a small telescope, and, on a nebulous background, more than two thousand to the same instrument armed with the camera. It is estimated that the chances in favor of at least the leading stars being a physical system are as 500,000 to one : some say as 500,000,000 to one. No matter which estimate you take—they both mean the same thing, viz., the incredible and so the unscientific.

The members of this group must therefore revolve about their common centre of gravity; and that means a revolution about this centre of all the solar families belonging to the system. Each family swings about its sun, and then each sun with its cortegé goes swinging about the common centre. More than this. If we examine a good map of the group we find several sub-groups in it, each of which must have its own centre of revolution. Alcyone forms a sub-group with several other small stars, Pleione and Atlas another, Asterope and some small stars another, perhaps Maia, Taygeta, and Celæno another. This means for every Solar family contained in the group at least three different revolutions going on at the same time : so that if one of the planets could leave a permanent luminous trail behind it its course would appear anything but an orbit. The complicate spiral would, however, appear considerably more symmetrical than that of the man who attempts to serve both God and Mammon at the same time, or to please all parties by the course he takes in social and political matters.

This beautiful group, named time out of mind, and, time out of mind, famous in poem and song, is remarkable for containing the largest star yet known to us, viz., ALCYONE. It must be equal to 12,000 such suns as ours to shine as it does at the distance from us of some 50 millions sun-distances. If brought within our system it would look our sun out of countenance in a moment. Our king of day would be scarcely more than a fire fly in the presence of that august monarch that blazes away in the neck of Taurus. He is worthy to be the central sun of the Milky Way—as the illustrious Maedler (himself a multiple star) thought him, and as time may yet prove him to the satisfaction of the scientific Thomases. We say *him*, though we have said *it*. Alcyone is a most masculine world though free of the neuter gender and bearing a feminine name.

# XIII.

## SOLAR COMMUNITIES—II.

PROVINCES.

CITIES.

XIII.

# SOLAR COMMUNITIES—II.

PROVINCES—CITIES.

Besides little knots or clumps of dwellings so closely set together that at a little distance they appear as one; besides the dwellings scattered at considerable intervals over a township and yet bound up together in one town system of government ; besides these, dwellings are sometimes largely accumulated in a city so that to an observer from without all individuality is lost, save toward the outskirts. From whatever point viewed, it is a maze of structures—heaps on heaps, by thousands and tens of thousands, with no possibility of distinguishing one home from another. And could the outside of every home be brilliantly illuminated in the night, as only plentiful electricity could do, we should see the city as a central blaze of light gradually thinning off toward the edges and there replaced by separated gleams which separate more and more till all is unbroken darkness.

Lifting our eyes to the sky we discover there celestial *cities*—as well as celestial townships and hamlets. We find stars in great bunches—apparently so packed and wedged together that in parts no telescope can separate them. At once we see that giants are before us, immense aggregations of suns, huge centres of condensed population ; that each cluster must count its shining families by tens and perhaps hundreds of thousands, were it possible to count them. And each cluster is plainly a neighborhood by itself. All around it is comparative, if not absolute, vacancy. It is insulated. And the interval between it and other like shining islands is much greater than between groups. Its appearance is just what a city whose houses are all in a vivid glow would present in the blackest of nights. I say *its appearance*. Of course the closeness of the stars to one another is only apparent. They must be actually hundreds of millions of miles apart ; and they appear otherwise chiefly because, being disposed in solid forms, they are projected on one another.

Some groups of stars can be recognized as such by the naked eye. But no cluster, no celestial city, appears as such save in a telescope. In a few cases a good eye may detect a small hazy spot which when viewed through a telescope turns out to be a nest or swarm of suns ; but generally such swarms do not even hint their existence save to our better instruments. The larger and better our instruments the more of these clusters do we find. Sir William Herschel made out a list of more than one hundred, and since his time many more have been noted. His son alone added more than fifty to the list. What a happy thing when a son succeeds to the successes and glory of his father! A hundred years have passed since the great father of observational astronomy disappeared, but his soul is still marching on. Doubtless the next hundred years (which none of us will live to see through) will harvest a great addition to our already splendid catalogue of celestial cities. Men go, but discoveries and men continue to come. City-annexes in our day are fashionable.

Hitherto I have spoken only of those clusters which are partly resolved into separate stars by the telescope. Some of these were, at first and for a long time, supposed to be no clusters at all ; were declared to have an irresolvable aspect ; were confidently pronounced vast clouds of fiery gas and vapor. But, one by one, they have opened and spread out their glittering units under the searching gaze of greater refractors and reflectors. Parsonstown has done wonders. This en-

13

courages us to think that still further telescopic improvement will show the stellar character of other cloud-like celestial objects to which this character is still stoutly refused by some.

But the telescope is not the only finder of clusters. The spectroscope is even more powerful. It can out-travel and out-search the best object glass or speculum that ever went hunting through the spaces. Rosse's great mirror is but an infant to it. And it has shown that some 4000 cloudlets on which our telescopes make no impression as analysts are really clusters of stars ; for it gets from them the continuous spectrum of solids or liquids. And, though another 4000 cloudlets give the bright-lined spectrum of gases, this does not prove that even they do not consist of separate stars, because some separate stars (for example, those in the Trapezium of Orion) also give the gaseous spectrum. Men sometimes lose their character by going into society ; not so the stars.

The islands in the ocean, while showing a general tendency to roundness, give us specimens of almost every form and internal aspect. It is so with our cities. Generally roundish and densest toward the centre they yet appear in every variety of shape and apparent structure. They are oval, square, crescent, fan-shaped, ring-shaped (parks in

the middle and elsewhere), irregular beyond de-
scription. Ancient cities ended abruptly with
walls, and all was vacuity beyond. Modern cities
are apt to pass out gradually into straggling
suburbs : now the densest part has this shape and
now it has that, now it is here and now it is there.
The same variety is found among the island-
cities of the stars. Some are accurately globular ;
most of them are roundish, with stars compacted
most toward the centre and thinning away gradually toward the edges where they are sparsely
sown ; but we have specimens of almost every
conceivable form and internal aspect. Thus, in
the cluster known as 30 Doradûs, the nucleus appears as a rough silver backbone, with strong
spurs from either side, in the midst of an assemblage of scattered stars spread out like wings.
Also, the Crab Cluster in Taurus is named from
the fact that the bright streams of condensation
were supposed to resemble a crab. The astronomical fathers might have found a more dignified
comparison ; but the people who had the naming
of things in the sky did not stop for trifles.

This variety of shape and structure does not
show the absence of law and order among the sky-
cities whose houses and palaces are suns ; but it
does show that the Supreme knows how to make a

host of celestial families dwell harmoniously together under a wide variety of conditions. The government of cities is the problem of our civilization, and a hard one. We cannot boast of our success in dealing with it. Our New Yorks and Chicagos are not as well regulated as they might be, if we may trust the outcry against them. There would be no call for outcry were they as well governed as are those great celestial cities above us where God is the Mayor, Common Council, and Board of Aldermen.

How far away are the stellar clusters? This is one of the many questions which we cannot as yet definitely answer. No parallax of any cluster has yet been found. If none *can* be found, then the nearest is farther away than Capella whose light comes to us in about seventy years : and the most remote, viz., those just brought to view by the most powerful instrument, must be enormously farther away.

As to the number of suns contained in some of these clusters—it can afford comparison with the census of the greatest modern cities. Some, covering only about one-tenth of the space on the sky occupied by our moon, and near enough to be resolvable by small telescopes, contain not far from 20,000 suns each : how much greater must be the number in those clusters that are barely resolved by our largest telescopes, and yet cover several times as much space on the vault as does the moon!  There must be millions on millions in each of them.

And how enormous must be the spaces occupied by such metropolitan clusters?  If each of the 20,-000 suns of the cluster in Hercules is, on the average, as far from its nearest neighbor as we are from the nearest star, the diameter of the cluster would be about thirty times the distance of Alpha Centauri from us.  If this cluster were carried away 500 times its present distance, its apparent size would be only one 25,000th part of the moon's disc; and only one 250,000th part of the size of some of the resolved clusters.

The stars in these mighty swarms, being more widely separated from other stars than they are from one another, of course form as many systems by themselves ; in each of which all the stars are moving about a common centre of gravity as well as about, it maybe, a hundred other sub-centres of revolution.  None of these revolutions, however, have been detected.  How could they, at distances so tremendous that the sun might move thousands of millions of miles without seeming to move at all ?  The time, however, may come when a com-

parison of photographic charts made at very long
intervals will reveal changes.   Centuries will go
and discoveries will come.   The march of time
will show the march of stars within clusters and
the march of clusters themselves.   The force of
gravity must keep everything in the heavens on
the move.

In this respect the itinerant cities in the heavens
differ from cities on the earth.   The latter are
fastened to one spot.    They never go on pilgrim-
age.   Transference is to them destruction.   Old
Tyre may become New Tyre, Thebes may become
Memphis and Memphis become Cairo, but it is
only by passing through the jaws of dissolution.
But the celestial cities that from age to age seem
to occupy precisely the same place are really
locomotive beyond anything seen on earth.   We
have seen cities lifted to a drier level ; have seen
single buildings, in a somewhat ragged state,
creeping along our streets to a new site ; but we
have never seen, and never will see, Jerusalem
transferred to Chicago.

Most cities look well at a distance.   In the con-
fused mass of structures that meets the eye the
ugly and mean fail to appear, while over all tower
the domes and spires of temples and palaces,
perhaps warm and golden in the glow of a setting

sun. Celestial cities also look well at our distance. Some of them could hardly look better. It is not easy to imagine in them anything unworthy or even common place. The magnificence is so pure, so sweet, so intense, so overflowing. Look, for example, at the Clusters in Capricornus, Libra, Perseus, and especially at that in Hercules. It is visible as a faint haze to the naked eye, appears as a small round comet to a small telescope, but in a powerful instrument breaks up into thousands of stars running up into a blaze at the centre. This is the Cluster on which, as seen in his great reflector, Sir William Herschel went into a sort of astronomical rapture. He describes himself as almost leaping with wonder and delight as the glorious spectacle burst upon him. And he a gray-beard and a philosopher to boot! And yet, no one who has seen under favorable circumstances that blazing city of God, would have blamed the venerable philosopher if he had actually done what he was sorely tempted to do.

Two of the clusters just mentioned are globular—are accurately round and their light gradually increases toward the centre as it would do if the stars were pretty equally distributed through a globular space. Another globular cluster (47 Toucani) of great splendor was observed by Sir John

Herschel in the Southern Hemisphere. He wrote of it : " A stupendous object—a most magnificent globular cluster, completely insulated, upon a ground of the sky perfectly black." A mighty orb of gems of a pale rose color, all by itself in a deserted sky—an unruined Palmyra!

In the case of the binary and multiple stars the orbits are very elliptical, resembling those of comets. This fact is not yet well explained by the nebular hypothesis. But a still greater difficulty is found in the globular clusters. Of course, in such a cluster the orbits about a common centre must have to one another every degree of inclination ; and, indeed, whatever solid form a cluster may have its orbits must be very far from lying all in one plane. How can this be reconciled with the notion that the worlds in each cluster have all sprung from one central rotation ? Sir John Herschel called attention to this in the following words :

" If the theory (nebular) be regarded as receiving the smallest support from any observed numerical relations which actually hold good among the elements of the planetary orbits, I beg leave to demur. Assuredly it receives no support from the observation of the effect of siderial aggregation as exemplified in the formation of globular and elliptic clusters. For we see this cause, working out in thousands of instances, to have resulted not in the formation of a single large central body surrounded by a few smaller attendants disposed in one plane around it, but in systems of infinitely greater complexity consisting of multitudes of nearly equal luminaries grouped together in solid globular or elliptic forms."

# XIV.

# SOLAR COMMUNITIES—III.

STATES.

EMPIRES.

## XIV.

# SOLAR COMMUNITIES—III.

STATES—EMPIRES.

Our terrestrial cities are found combined into States and Empires. Several populous centres, with boroughs and villages and hamlets and solitary homes interspersed, form one political system, subject to one central government, and separated from other similar systems by distinct boundaries.

In like manner several clusters of stars, with intermediate spaces occupied by stars in groups and multiples and units, are set in a single stellar system, under one central control, bound to "stand or fall together," and parted by well defined frontiers from other like systems. Let us call it a celestial empire. We shall find it large enough, and glorious enough, to deserve the name. Its clusters are celestial cities, while its groups of various grades are celestial boroughs and villages and hamlets sprinkled about with country homes.

In such a celestial empire, located far away, we would expect that sometimes nothing would appear to us save the clusters—the great condensed populous centres. Distance would completely quench the feebler intermediate illumination. It would be as when we look at the map of an earthly country reduced to a small scale. All the small places have disappeared. Nothing is seen but the larger cities. But we know that, between the New Yorks and Philadelphias and San Franciscos, lie concealed immense populations in thousands of smaller communities and in the scattered homes of mountain and forest and prairie. Other maps on a larger scale will show us smaller places ; but none will show us every lonely farmhouse, or even every hamlet, in the whole broad land, from ocean to ocean.

So we should expect that great celestial empires, reduced to a small scale by distance, would sometimes show us only a number of clusters in a neighborhood by themselves. Such cases are actually found. If these remote empires could be set in motion toward us the spaces between the clusters would gradually brighten, and at last we should see them populous with stars, solitary or in groups. We know it would be so, for the same change in appearance takes place as we successively enlarge the telescope brought to bear on them.

I say that such is the result in some cases. Still, in other cases, the result does not follow. We enlarge our instruments till they pierce the spaces like the immense refractor at Mt. Hamilton or even the immenser reflector at Birr Castle, and yet the black vacancies between the clusters give no sign of being peopled. Plainly they are *not* peopled. There are no intermediate groups and scattered stars. We have celestial cities only, composing our celestial empire. It is with some great states above as it anciently tended to be with all states below. For greater security men once gathered their homes in walled towns. From these they went forth to their farms in the morning and to them returned as evening drew on. The country side was almost empty of habitations. Away on the frontiers of history we see scarcely anything but Babylons and Ninevehs, Thebes' and Memphises; and no wonder, for there was little else to be seen.

We have found satellites in groups, planets in groups, suns in groups, and sun-groups in those still larger groups which we call clusters. This principle of organization, we would naturally expect to find continued. We should expect that clusters themselves would often appear in groups. And so they do—in groups of two and three and four and more, up to hundreds. In some of these the clusters are widely apart, while in others they crowd closely together and are seemingly connected by nebulous isthmuses. Sometimes one cluster seems partly to overlap another ; as would happen if one were partly between us and the other and so visually projected on it. In very many cases the different clusters so run together that the whole appear as one continuous bed of stars, only with several centres of special condensation—very much as certain neighboring cities we know of would appear to a bird's-eye view, and as would all the cities of some densely populated empire that we can imagine. In short, there is about the same variety as to number, size, shape, and relative position of the clusters composing a celestial empire as there is of the cities composing a terrestrial. The cities of terrestrial empires are of all sizes, from Londons downward. They are, or have been, of all numbers from two to thousands. They lie thousands of miles apart, or snug up to one another as do New York and Brooklyn. Brooklyn bridge first appeared in the skies, and the shining model is considerably stronger and more durable than the copy.

Of the hundreds of examples of grouped clusters that might be named, most would be scarcely more than names. They are so remote from us, we have to deal with them at so long a range, that our astronomical artillery, however skillfully plied, can bring down scarcely more than their position and compound character. So we will confine our attention to a few leading examples of the more interesting sort—beginning with some in which the clusters are in such close juxtaposition to one another that they are commonly reckoned as one cluster.

In the constellation *Vulpecula* is a cluster called the *Dumb Bell*, from its resemblance to a dumb bell. It really consists of two clusters joined to each other by a bridge of stars. It is easy to see from the shape of this compound cluster that each extreme of it must have its own centre of revolution, while both extremes must revolve about a common centre.

Another compound cluster is the *Crab Cluster* in Taurus. This cluster, like that just mentioned, for a time resisted analysis by the telescope, but has at length been resolved into stars. It consists of an oblong cluster to which on both sides are attached a number of nearly parallel streamers— the whole somewhat resembling a crab. The

14

streamers in some instances seem but feebly connected with the main cluster ; some are nearly equal to it in length ; and all of them are distinctly separated from one another. Each of these wisps or jets or spurs of stars must be of immense length, and have its own centre of revolution as well as one common to all of them and the main cluster. So the whole object must be astronomically plural. A city on earth can send out jets of population in any direction and to any length and yet the whole remain but one city. Not so a cluster. A river of suns, projected from the main cluster beyond a certain near point, would infallibly set up in business on its own account and establish for itself a new sub-centre of revolution, without forsaking the old.

The *ring cluster* in *Lyra*. This is one of several annular nebulæ, and easily chief of them all for size and beauty. Though giving the gaseous spectrum, it has been partly resolved into stars by the great telescope of the Earl of Rosse. Under this telescope it appears as a crown studded and fringed with jewelled points ; and within the crown appear several distinct streams of light. We have here a ring cluster inclosing several stream-like clusters.

A famous object is the great nebula in Andromeda. It is faintly visible to the naked eye. Under the telescope it appears as a group of six or
seven nebulæ of round or lenticular forms ; but, as
given by the more searching camera, it alters
much in appearance, though without losing its
composite character. We now see a vast and
extremely elliptical central body, somewhat mot-
tled as by various centres of condensation ; and
around it appear to stretch two or more concentric rings. On opposite sides of the rings and at
a considerable distance from them are two small
round nebulæ of about the same order of brightness. This compound nebula is thought by some
to have been resolved into stars by the telescope.
Others deny this ; but we must still regard the
nebula as a compound cluster because it gives the
continuous spectrum. The fact that, though just
visible to the naked eye, it requires the most powerful of telescopes to show it doubtfully as a
cluster, shows that it must be a very brilliant as
well as remote object. Also very large.

But there is a far larger and more noted nebula
than that in the girdle of Andromeda—also one
that seems to be a group of clusters. I mean the
great nebula in Orion. It covers several square
degrees of the sky, and is by far the most striking

nebula in the northern hemisphere. It is very irregular in form ; consists of numerous white patches of all shapes, connected with one another by bridges and isthmuses. Under the largest instruments, we have a large central nucleus that sends out many spiral streams and fan-like appendages, while at one side appear patches not connected with the main body. That it is a compound object is certain : that it is a compound cluster actually analyzed by the telescope has been repeatedly announced and as often contradicted ; that it consists, in part at least, of stellar clusters seems decided by the fact that a faint continuous spectrum has been seen in connection with its gaseous spectrum, while this last belongs to some undoubted clusters and separate stars. While looking at the "dark lanes and coal sacks" that divide up the nebula in all directions, it is easy to regard them as the vacancies between stellar swarms closely grouped, but still swarms having so much individuality that each must have its own centre of revolution as well as one common to the whole group.

Whirlpools on the earth are not as many as they once were. Where are Scylla and Charybdis? Where the mighty vortex made when great Atlantis suddenly sank in mid ocean? Where

the terrible Maelstrom on the coast of Norway
that frightened the geographical babes of the last
generation ? Even Hell Gate, to whose far-reach-
ing suction the sailors of New Amsterdam gave
such wide berth, is among the missing. All the
Vortices (including those of Descartes) seem to
have been translated and set up among the constellations. The nebula in the sword of Orion,
just spoken of, has in parts something of the
whirlpool look. But there are several other
nebulæ which have this look throughout, and so
go by the name of the spiral or whirlpool nebulæ.
These, for the most part, give the continuous
spectrum, and so are to be considered clusters.
But they are compound clusters. One in the
Triangle shows at least five distinct centres of
condensation ; another in Ursa Major shows a
dozen or more ; another in Leo is like two slender
cones, built of concentric layers and set base
toward base on opposite sides of a system of concentric rings inclosing a cluster—the whole resembling somewhat a gigantesque and arabesque
unstrung bow fit for giant Orion himself. But
the most striking example is what is known as the
*Whirlpool Nebula of Lord Rosse.* This is in *Canes
Venatici.* It shows conspicuously two round clusters : and to the larger of these are attached,

generally very feebly, many clusters, distinctly
separated from one another, in the form of
streamers that seem to issue from it in jets and
torrents of suns, and then to be driven about it as
the long tresses of a woman in a gale might be
blown about her head. In addition to these swirls
of clusters there are several straight ones. The
whole aspect suggests a celestial empire of vast
complexity whose multitudinous sub-centres of
revolution are carried about one common gravity-
centre of the whole.

It is common, now, to assume that nebulæ giving the bright-lined spectrum are not clusters
of stars, but vast continuous masses of gas not
yet individualized into suns. Of course there *may*
be such gaseous masses in the distant heavens,
since we know some in the Solar System in the
form of comets and meteor-swarms (these, however, are not self luminous) ; but it is certain that
the gaseous spectrum given by certain nebulæ
does not PROVE that they are not clusters ; for it is
admitted that some resolved clusters and separate
stars do the same. What is shown is merely that,
if the nebula is a cluster, its separate stars are gaseous. In this state of the case we are entitled to
assume that at least a proportion of the nebulæ in
a large group of them are clusters, though giving
the bright-lined spectrum.

# XV.

## Solar Communities—IV.

### Specimen Empire.

IV.

# SOLAR COMMUNITIES—IV.

SPECIMEN EMPIRE.

But can we not do better than this? Have we no example of a celestial empire so near to us, and so familiar to both optical instruments and the naked eye, as to throw a flood of light on the structure and condition of those brother empires whose banners and coats of arms are only just visible in our mightiest instruments, and whose remoteness from us dwarfs them into mystery and almost into practical non-existence?

We can answer in the affirmative. Fortunately, we find ourselves placed in the very midst of such an empire; and can closely examine it as a specimen of the more distant firmaments. I mean the

MILKY WAY.

The faintly luminous band across the sky which goes by this name, and with which everybody, from Adam downward, has been familiar, has been found to be not only a vast congregation of stars but a congregation of clusters. Hundreds of clus-

ters are found in it; and between and around these
are all grades of stellar groups, down to stars that
seem like hermits amid deserts of space. And the
whole glorious aggregation of worlds is a system
by itself. It has distinct boundaries. It is really
an island with vast unoccupied stretches of space
all around it. Astronomers differ among themselves as to some features of this island; but not
as to its *being* an island subject to one central control.

Now let us state what is known, or reasonably
conjectured, of this specimen celestial empire—
with its mighty cities, its populous boroughs, its
radiant towns and villages and hamlets, its lonely
homes gleaming far away from neighbors among
the solitudes of the celestial country-side.

To the naked eye the Milky Way looks like a
ragged whitish belt, passing completely around the
sky, so as to divide it into two nearly equal hemispheres. At a certain point this belt parts into
two streams which, after remaining apart for nearly
half its course, come together again. Under our
telescopes all parts of the zone break up into
throngs of stars: as our instruments sweep away
to the right or left, the dense masses thin away
gradually into separate stars which at last come
to be few and far between—like the angel visits of

which we have heard, and in which we ought so heartily to believe. Though brighter at some points than at others, and generally brighter in the Southern Hemisphere than in the Northern, yet, on the whole and considering all circumstances, the belt appears not very uneqally luminous in all parts of the heavens; while to the right and left of it the scattered stars appear in about equal numbers.

Now for an *hypothesis*—that mysterious and wonderful thing that plays so conspicuous a part in modern researches! Yes, an *hypothesis* is the first thing to be looked up when we come across anything on earth or in the heavens that needs explanation. Whether in politics or science or religion, the only recognized way out of difficulties in these days is to get an hypothesis, a sufficient hypothesis, the only sufficient hypothesis; to work upon them. In the present case, Sir William Herschel has gotten the start of us and made ready to our hand an hypothesis which, for a hundred years, has had the general assent of astronomers as being the sufficient, and the only sufficient explanation of those aspects of the Milky way which I have just mentioned. And here it is.

Let us suppose that we are situated not very far from the centre of a bed of stars having roughly the shape of a grindstone, whose thickness is much less than its length—a grindstone deeply cloven along nearly half its round, into two equal parts which are set at a small angle to each other. In that case we should see a Milky Way in our sky having precisely the same features we now notice. Accordingly, astronomers now generally allow that the supposition is a picture, in a rough way, of the actual fact, and that all the separate stars visible throughout the entire heavens must belong to our Milky Way system.

So much for the *general shape of our Empire*—which is agreed to all the more readily because we find almost its exact duplicate, cleavage and all, in a nebula near the tail of *Ursa Major*.

What is the *size* of our empire? An evident way of approximating to this would be to look off at right angles to the general plane of the Milky Way with gradually increasing telescopic powers, and notice at what power new stars cease to appear: we then have reached the frontier in that direction. Doing the same in the direction of the length, we have reached the frontier in that direction. On comparing these two frontier·powers we have the ratio of the thickness of the stratum to its length. This ratio the elder Herschel, making careful soundings through the stellar deeps, estimated to be as 1 to 22. It remains to get some idea of the absolute value of the unit representing the half-thickness of the stratum. This value he estimated at 40 times the distance from us of stars of the first magnitude. But astronomers now reckon this distance to be, on the average, about 15 years of light-travel. This makes the thickness about 1,200 years and its length 26,000.

These views of the elder Herschel are now questioned. While all astronomers believe that our stellar empire has its boundaries, and that its length greatly exceeds its thickness, some will have it that it has never yet been seen through in any direction, that our most powerful telescope, that carries the sight 500 times deeper into space than the naked eye penetrates (that is 60,000 years of light travel) has not yet reached the lateral frontier, much less the rim of our celestial grind-stone. This makes its whole length at least 120,-000 years—which means that, if a ray of light were to start this moment from the frontier and proceed diametrically across at a steady pace of 186,-000 miles a second, it would take a small eternity to reach the other side. Whatever modifications in such figures future researches may make, they are not likely to leave our celestial empire appreciably less astounding in the extent of its territory.

As to the *number of stars* contained in this vast territory, we are in very much the same situation as we are in with reference to the population of our world. The estimates of experts differ greatly. Some tell us that 800 millions will sum up all lands; others affirm almost double this number. Some will have it that China alone contains 600 millions; while others say this estimate is monstrous and lessen it by one-half. And who *can* know how many people unexplored Africa contains? And yet we know that the world's population is immense; and that, in general, the tendency of increased knowledge of our planet has been to larger and larger estimates. The census of our celestial empire has varied similarly. It has long been understood that its stars must be reckoned by millions. As to how many millions, astronomers do not find it easy to agree. When stars are projected on one another in great heaps, beyond the analysis of any telescope, an estimate of their number must be very rough indeed. Some say 18 millions—this is the lowest figures. Some say 100 millions—this is the highest. Whether the highest is high enough is still an open question.

In any view, what an immense congregation of suns and Solar Systems! What an enormous Celestial Empire! Glorious cities by the hun-

dreds! Glorious boroughs and villages by the
thousands and tens of thousands! Glorious hamlets and units by millions and tens of millions!
And then the radiant families of habitable planets
that doubtless hide by the hundreds of millions
behind the veiling glory of transcendent suns!

Of course, every individual orb of this wonderful
host, while tracing out at the same time a wilder-
ness of sub-orbits about local centres of many
orders, is in motion about the common centre of
gravity of the whole system. Where is that common centre? Both Argelander and Maedler under-
took to answer this question—one locating the
centre in Perseus, the other in Taurus near
Alcyone the brightest of the Pleiades. The latter
view has had the larger acceptance. Supposing it
to be the true view, now is it consistent with the
generally admitted fact that our sun is located not
far from the centre of the Milky Way? The
answer may be that the space-centre of a stellar
system is not necessarily the centre of gravity;
and that, if the two are practically coincident in
our system, yet both our sun and Alcyone may be
relatively near the united centre—the distance
between the two being very trifling compared with
their distance from the frontiers; and the orbit of
our sun, however imposing in itself, being a mere

nothing compared with the orbits of frontier suns. Our orbit, it is true, is no small matter considered by itself; for our sun has been moving at the rate of about 100 millions of miles a year toward the Constellation Hercules without deviating sensibly from a straight line for an entire century. What a vast orbit that must be whose curve rounds so slowly at such bewildering speed!

Such is our sample celestial empire. In it we find from 20 to 100 millions of suns, in singles and multiples and groups and clusters, sown over such enormous spaces that light itself, that miracle-traveler, could only cross them in thousands upon thousands of years ; all wheeling in incessant and mighty movement, not only about the centre of gravity of the whole, but also about an indefinite number of sub-centres, and yet in the bonds of a glorious order and harmony that seem to be in-destructible save by the fiat of the Eternal. Do we not see here an example of what those other celestial empires are which we have named, and seen to be, empires but whose vast remove from us hides so much from our struggling and im-patient sight ?

It is proper to say that some astronomers think that all visible nebulæ belong to our Milky Way system and are contained within it. That some nebulous masses, like the comets and meteor-swarms of our Solar System, may be mixed up with the discrete stars is certainly very possible ; and, as soon as good evidence can be shown that such is the case, there is no difficulty in the world in receiving it. But the evidence is not yet satisfactory : and if it were, what a leap to the conclusion that *all* nebulæ are within the Milky Way ! We need a bridge for so great a chasm. Is there any ?

If the Milky Way were carried away from us 300 times its length it would appear as a medium-sized nebula. As yet the actual distance from us of not a single cluster or nebula has been determined : but it would seem that all irresolvable cluster-nebulæ *must* lie greatly beyond the remotest separate star discoverable by our largest telescope, or its camera, and *may* lie so far away as to imply in many a magnitude fully equal to that of the Milky Way.

If a cluster-nebula is at the same distance from us as a given separate star it will appear resolved. Hence, if it does not show resolution, it must be more remote. If that separate star is the faintest one visible in the camera of the largest telescope, the nebula must be more remote than that star. So all the cluster nebulæ as yet unresolvable are

15

more remote than the remotest star yet seen by our most powerful instruments, and that star is 60,000 years away, as flies the light.

More remote—but how much more remote ? A double star whose constituents are equal gives twice the light of each ; a sextuple star whose constituents are equal would give six fold the light of each. And so on. If a cluster nebula is so remote that the light of 100 lateral stars appear as one, that light is 100 times that of each constituent star ; and this manifold light is still further increased by contributions of rays from all the stars of the swarm that fill the background to an indefinite distance. And this is not all the increase ; for, as Humboldt observes, " the retina retains a less vivid impression of separate than of infinitely near luminous points," so that, if there were no blending of lateral and background rays, a crowded swarm of stars would always be seen much further than any single constituent member could be. Hence, a cluster containing millions of stars that just begins to show resolution at the border or other thin parts under the most powerful telescope, must be far brighter on the whole than the faintest star that appears in the same instrument ; and may be bright enough to be visible to the naked eye (as is the nebula in

Andromeda), even if carried away much further into the abyss and made irresolvable by our present instruments. All irresolvable clusters are more distant than the most distant star yet seen: and those of them that, on the whole, are still *far* brighter in the Parsonstown reflector than such star must be *far* more remote. The clusters we have instanced are of this sort. Who can show that the Herschels and Maedlers and Lockyers were wrong in regarding them as external galaxies ? Let the old view hold its place till a clear better can lay claim to it. The king should not retire till a lawful successor can be found. A vacuum is against nature. A vacant throne means disorder, anxiety, in short, anarchy. And anarchy is intolerable in both politics and science.

# XVI.

## SOLAR COMMUNITIES—V.

### FEDERATED EMPIRES.

✦

## XVI.

# SOLAR COMMUNITIES—V.

FEDERATED EMPIRES.

Our earthly cities, with their intermediate bor-oughs and villages and hamlets, are gathered into states and empires. And empires themselves, especially in these days, are often federated to-gether for special objects. Our fathers saw several great European Powers leagued together against Napoleon. To-day we have a Triple Alliance, for purposes best known to themselves, between Germany, Austria, and Italy: also, a still more noteworthy alliance between eighteen distinct Governments against the destroyers of Africa. And we are hoping that the time is not far distant (would that it would arrive to-day) when all the great empires of civilization will band themselves to settle all international disputes by peaceful arbitration. Greatest and most auspicious of all federations (save one)—we hail the growing sound of thy chariot wheels and the growing flashes of thy torches! Will they not arrive to-morrow?

Lift your eyes. You shall see not only celestial cities, with their intermediate communities, gathered into celestial empires; but you shall also see celestial empires grouped together in a grander federation. We would naturally expect to see this grander order of things, we who have ascended through so many orders of groups—satellite-groups, planet-groups, sun-groups, cluster-groups—surely we might reasonably predict that we would find the cluster-groups themselves, which we have chosen to call empires, gathered into groups more or less large, occupying one local neighborhood, bound together by special ties of mutual attraction, and sweeping in still grander curves than any we have yet seen about a still mightier centre of gravity. Even if we cannot actually find such federated empires, we must still believe that they exist beyond our sight. Otherwise Nature is not of a piece. The heavens are not built throughout on the same plan. All the analogies are defied and disappointed.

But federated celestial empires, though far away, are not beyond sight. What are the Magellanic Clouds? The voyager in the Southern Hemisphere looks toward the Pole and sees two masses of luminous haze—the larger, called *Nubecula Major*, covering a space about 200 times that

occupied by the moon, the other, *Nubecula Minor*
measuring considerably less. If that voyager happens to be Sir John Herschel with his telescope,
both these luminous clouds open up and become
two vast collections of clusters and nebulæ, near
to each other but separated by wide Saharas from
other clusters. In the larger Nubecula a powerful telescope reveals 278 clusters, and nebulæ that
may be clusters: in the smaller the collection is
less large and brilliant but still imposing, and
near it is Toucan one of the grandest clusters in
the whole heavens. Taking into account only
known or probable clusters, we have here two
immense celestial empires in juxtaposition, forming one system, bound to stand or fall together,
wheeling in stupendous revolution about a common centre. Two clusters in one system, and
nine in the other, are specially noteworthy on account of their being of about the same order of
brightness and so more clearly in the same local
neighborhood.

In the constellation Virgo there is an immense
assembly of nebulæ. Most of them are only visible in large telescopes. They lie in groups of all
sizes, from two to scores and hundreds. At one
point 13 nebulæ appear within two degrees of one
another. At another point 300 nebulæ cross the

field of a fixed telescope in a single hour. Sometimes two groups make a neighborhood by themselves; sometimes a much larger number enter
into the federation. By twos and threes and scores
are the groups profusely sown through this populous region.

Here we have, not merely groups of clusters,
but clusters of groups. Here we have, not merely
a number of clusters composing a celestial empire,
but a number of empires bound up together into
one system by local neighorhood and the meshes
of mutual attraction and a common centre of revolution. A nest of star-nests? Yes. A bed of
star-beds? Yes; and more. What we see is a
coalition, not of cities, but of States. It is a grand
confederation above, answering to an international
confederation below in virtue of which the flags
and armies of different countries come together
and camp and march side by side for a common
purpose. We have seen clusters in partnership
with clusters; now we see a congeries of clusters
in partnership (in some cases a partnership close
enough to be called a marriage) with another congeries. The principle of association binds together
aggregates as well as individuals. Empires crave
fellowship as well as families. Not a star but belongs to some stellar community; not a stellar

community (save one) but joins hands with other stellar communities of the same order. And so the complication goes on, in ever ascending orders, as far as our present sight carries us, and doubtless goes on still till that Universe System is reached which can have no fellow.

These federated empires in Virgo belong to a nebulous zone lying nearly at right angles to the Milky Way. In this zone most of the nebulæ are found, not continuously, but broken up as it were into separate camps. The grandest of these is the one just considered; but others of great interest are found; especially in Leo, Ursa Major, Coma Berenicis, and Pisces Boreales. The appearance is as it would be if thousands of Milky Ways were carried off vast stretches beyond our Milky Way till they became faint round spots in the largest telescopes, and were then disposed about us in great detached assemblages. Each of these is a system of federated empires. And the whole broken baldric of firmaments is itself only another larger unit of celestial organization, as we advance toward that last most mysterious and yet most certain *Unit*, which includes within itself the whole material cosmos with its unspeakable centre of gravity, revolution, and government.

I say "that most certain *Unit.*" For, that the whole sum of worlds is itself a unit whose parts are correlated to one another in a grand harmony of stable movement and result, under one central government whose steady and potential hand men sometimes call eternal law, cannot reasonably be doubted by anyone who has fairly considered those smaller units which have gone on enlarging and ascending under the eye of science. Does this ascent of orders end where our vision at present happens to end? No logician will venture an affirmative. No experienced astronomer, who is at the same time a believer in an architecture of the heavens, but is abundantly prepared to feel that the sublime ascent of orders still continues behind the scenes, through we know not how many steps, until at last the universe system is reached—that system of celestial empires that is all comprehending and so can have no fellow; that congeries of firmaments that stands in its lonely vastness and reverently says after its Maker the great words "I am, and besides me there is none else."

But our observation, though not our faith, is yet far enough from this point. The Milky Way of nebulæ, bounds our present vision. But we hope, before long, to see some of those fellow systems

which federate with it into a still higher whole.
Our telescopes will become more penetrating.
Our spectroscopes will sound the abyss with a still
longer and surer line. Our cameras will send us
cablegrams across still wider oceans, picturing still
more stupendous continents. Our present instru-
mental university will take on large annexes that
will double its efficiency. Invention is already
wide awake. Discovery is already on tiptoe of
outlook and expectation. The past encourages
and the future beckons. The known is full of
prizes ; and the larger unknown cannot be poorer,
nay, must be richer. Fame awaits the enterprising
explorer. Riches await him. And he cries out to
his fellows, "Forward comrades, to new conquests!
Down with all barriers! Up with all curtains!"
Certainly audacity is not wanting to the spirit of
the age. And fortune will favor the brave. Faith
in success will win it. Time and genius and
bright-eyed hope will more and more master the
situation. Standing on the shoulders of the fathers we shall see greater horizons. The next century, now just at hand, will stand twenty stories
from the ground, and will be able to look far
beyond them all. How far? Certainly not to
the frontiers of the shining hosts of suns and systems. Ah, who but the all-knowing Eternal

knows whether there be any frontiers? But far
enough to make signal additions to the glory of
that temple which science is building for wonder
and worship.

In our knowlege of natural science almost any
amount of enlargement may reasonably be expected with the advancing years. But we cannot
expect a like enlargement in our religious knowledge. All the great religious facts, doctrines, and
duties are already written in the hearts of men
and in a Book. Both records are closed. No additions will be made to either of them. Some few
passages in each may get a better interpretation—
also a worse. On minor points of the Bible (very
few indeed) some additional light may be thrown
—also additional darkness. But not a single new
doctrine or duty will, by any amount of talent and
research, be added to that great stock of religious
information—contained in the Bible. The advancing years will never carry us beyond the Apos-
tles. The bruit of alleged first-class discoveries
will come to us, as it has every now and then come
in the past ; men will cry their *Ecces* and *Eurekas*
to us in triumphal tones, and claim that they have
left the old Bible far behind; but their discoveries
will turn out to be inventions, their science fables,
their novelties "doctrines of devils." The role of

an extra-Biblical discoverer in religion is an abom-
ination. We like courage in the explorer of new
lands: we have nothing but commendation for
every Columbus who audaciously launches away
from the coasts of our present astronomy into new
abysses in search of new worlds; but, in religious
matters, I take my stand on Holy Scripture and
ask for the *old* paths of both doctrine and duty,
confident that no others will give either truth or
"rest to the soul."

But it is otherwise in the domain of natural science. Any day may bring magnificent additions
to our astronomy. A few years will be almost
sure to bring them. And, when they come, may
you and I be there to see and welcome them. We
will welcome them, partly because of the intellectual pleasure, the mental enlargement, and the
various contributions which such new knowledge
will make, directly or indirectly, to the comforts
and ornaments of our civilization; but, chiefly,
because of the strong light which it can, if properly used, be made to throw on the great religious
truths already revealed. It will give us no new
religious truth, but it will, to fair and candid
usage, furnish means for illustrating the old. I
say "if properly used." Knowledge has always
been a sword with which a man may slay others

and himself; as well as sustain law, resist oppression, and save life—has always been an electric light which can blind and burn and kill; as well as turn night into day, peril into safety, and the lost into the found.   The more a man knows the more harm he can do.   The better equipped Satan is the worse for the world.   Would that he were an ignoramus, and a weak one!   We could defeat him more easily.

# XVII.

## ASTRONOMICAL RELIGION—I.

REALITY OF GOD.

HIS UNITY.

HIS PERSONAL GREATNESS.

16

## XVII.

# ASTRONOMICAL RELIGION—I.

HIS REALITY—HIS UNITY—HIS PERSONAL GREATNESS.

That some persons, well acquainted with the main astronomical facts, never actually get any religious help from them is among the plainest of facts. *Circumspice!*

Some distinctly claim that this is as it should be —that, really, neither Astronomy nor any other science has anything to say on the subject of religion; that it neither testifies for nor against; that it neither helps nor hinders, but is quite neutral, in that great conflict between the friends and enemies of religion that has been going on from the beginning, and is waxing so hot in our own times. In the view of these agnostics, the two realms of reason and faith, of science and religion, are so exceedingly far apart that there can be no serviceable communication between them. They are on opposite sides of the *Cosmos.* They are so unlike in their objects, evidences, and processes of reasoning that—Well, what has the zenith to do with the nadir?

Still others claim that Astronomy, as well as other sciences, has something to say on religious matters. but that what it has to say is positively unfriendly—especially to the religion of the Bible. They tell us that, while all sorts of scientific study indispose to a belief in the miraculous events which enter so largely and fundamentally into our Scriptures, the study of the heavens does so in a notable degree by the majesty of its lessons on the extent and constancy of the laws of Nature. And, further, they assure us that the mighty extent and glory of the universe as lately revealed by our researches, and the relatively insignificant place which the earth and man occupy in it, make it incredible that Deity should make so much account of us as the Scriptures represent; and especially that He should, in his own person, bring us such a scheme of redemption as we find woven into the whole fabric of Christianity. They are quite ready to adopt the language of the Psalmist, "When I consider thy heavens the work of thy fingers, the moon and the stars which thou hast ordained, what is man that thou art mindful of him, and the son of man that thou visitest him!" What is it but snatching a weapon from the Christian armory wherewith to assail the armory itself?

But there are others who, in the name of science itself as well as of religion, strongly deny these infidel and agnostic claims. The great astronomical sermons of Dr. Chalmers will not soon be forgotten. Nor, it is to be hoped, will that formal manifesto by 617 English scientists, many of whom were of the first eminence, expressing "sincere regret that researches into scientific truth are perverted by some in our own times into occasions for casting doubt on the truth and authenticity of the Holy Scriptures." Such men cannot allow that the Nature that speaks so eloquently to every other point of the compass becomes dumb as soon as it faces religion. If at no other time, Memnon must sound when he faces the sunrising. Much less can they allow that Astronomy and the Book are two opposite poles that defy and exasperate each other. On the contrary, they maintain that the two are mutually friendly and helpful in a high degree. "The undevout astronomer is mad" was the feeling of Kepler and Newton and Sir John Herschell; and it is still the feeling of not a few intelligent gazers at the heavens. They allow that the two fields are not exactly coterminous, that at certain points there is considerable interval between them; but they contend that they are always within speaking distance of each other, that they are always connected by by-ways and highways, if not by Milky Ways, that even as worlds throw light on other worlds across vast spaces, and sciences illustrate other sciences though differing as much as physics and metaphysics, even so does Astronomy shed light on Religion, however far apart in some respects the two may be.

With these latter views we heartily sympathize. It would seem that no one who believes in God, as being the author of both the astronomical heavens and the Bible, can doubt that there is a subtle harmony between them in virtue of which they must on the whole be mutually helpful when normally used. We are in the habit of thinking that works of the same author will throw light on one another. Accordingly, we believe that Astronomy contains very great help, not only for people already religious, in the way of illustrating, emphasizing, and enlarging their faith, but also for those who are yet so unfortunate as to be unbelievers of the most radical type. That it has been used in the service of the enemy we know. That its look faithward has sometimes been grim as death we allow. That it has made some shocking mistakes in favor of even materialism and atheism we cannot deny. That it is by no means equal in the religious service it renders to the Ten Commandments, or to prayer, or to the preaching of the Gospel, must be conceded to the evangelicals. At the same time it is a powerful auxiliary to them all. Though not an irresistible friend, nor the chief of friends, nor a friend that does not need to be guided and cultivated and discriminated from counterfeits, nor a friend who as mayor of the palace includes in himself all the royal powers and functions, it is still a friend well worth the having—especially as suggesting, illustrating, and emphasizing the following lessons.

1. *God is real.*—Some scientists deny this proposition on astronomical grounds. They say that the evolution of worlds by merely natural forces and laws is a matter of established science—that inasmuch as the nebular hypothesis will fully account for everything we find in the heavens without calling in the aid of the Supernatural, it is unphilosophical and unreasonable to go outside of Nature for its explanation.

The Christian should not be surprised at such an attitude as this. The Scriptures have forewarned him. These men do not see God in the heavens, not because He is not there, but because of spiritual blindness—of a certain indisposition and inaptitude toward religious things, which is a part of the natural depravity we all inherit and some cultivate. Atheistic astronomers are such by cultivation, and a plenty of it. "They did not *like* to retain God in their knowledge "— this is the open secret of their position. Atheism is in the hearts of men before it is in their intellect. Like the infernal Phlegethon, after leaving its occult source it runs for awhile beneath ground, and then debouches into view in hypotheses, speculations, arguments, evolutionisms, science falsely so called.

If it were otherwise—if these agnostical and atheistical men were really open-eyed with healthy vision, sincere inquirers after whatever truth is written on the spangled heavens'—nay, if they were only soundly converted men and, as such, had recovered in some good degree the original bias toward the true and holy, they would discover abundant evidence among the stars of the existence of a personal First Cause. Nature, then, would no longer seem to explain itself. It would be seen that blind atoms, by no possible hocus-pocus of combination and time, could become in the universe the equivalent of a Divine Framer and Governor—in short, that an undevout astronomer is mad.

This will seem a hard saying to some. But we make no apology for saying it ; for the Scriptures

have said it before us. "For the invisible things
of Him from the creation of the world are clearly
seen, being understood from the things that are
made, even his eternal power and Godhead : so
that they are without excuse." If the things that
are made, as known to the very heathen, leave
them without excuse for their ignorance of the
true God, how much more inexcusable must be
the atheists of our day amid the astounding reve-
lations of modern science, and especially amid
those hugest miracles of all that shine to them
under the name of astronomy ! Whoever declines
to allow it, and tells us of "honest doubt and
frank investigation ending in atheism," the
Christian is bound to say, "The heavens declare
the glory of God and the firmament showeth his
handy work."

"If the theory be regarded as receiving the
smallest support from any observed numerical relations which actually hold good among the
elements of the planetary orbits, I beg leave to
demur. Assuredly, it receives no support from
the observations of the effect of siderial aggregation as exemplified in the formation of globular
and elliptic clusters. For we see this cause, working out in thousands of instances, to have resulted
not in the formation of a single large central body

surrounded by a few smaller attendants disposed in one plane around it, but in systems of infinitely greater complexity, consisting of multitudes of nearly equal luminaries grouped together in solid globular or elliptic forms."

This testimony of Sir John Herschel, by far the most accomplished of English astronomers since Newton, to the insufficiency of the nebular hypothesis to account for the heavenly bodies, has been greatly strengthened by more recent researches. In fact, the hypothesis, so far as it proposes to explain the heavens without a Deity, has become so burdened with difficulties and insuperables that it no longer deserves serious consideration. The donkey, never strong, has quite broken down under his load. On the other hand, the only competing cosmogony, the Theistic, while perfectly sufficient and *a priori* at least as credible as any, is greatly the simplest, the surest, the safest, the sublimest, the most salutary, and the most in accordance with the convictions and traditions of mankind, especially of the most enlightened and moral part of mankind. In each of these respects it has almost infinitely the advantage over its competitor. And, according to the maxims and practice of philosophy in other things, such an aggregate superiority as this ought to cause

Theism to be promptly accepted and fully rested on as the true explanation of Nature. Whatever secular hypothesis could claim as much, would be accepted without hesitation by all impartial men. It would be considered triumphantly established. No scientist, with a reputation to lose, would for one moment think of venturing on opposition. On the contrary, an hypothesis so strongly fortified with veri-similitudes and superiorities over all rivals, would ascend the throne of faith and robe itself in the purple of all her prerogatives by unanimous acclamation of the Baconian philosophy, of scientific usage, and of the entire college of scholarly men.

Our space will not allow us to particularize the elaborate adaptation of means to ends that may be found in the mechanism of the heavens. They can be found in the works of Paley, Dick, and many others. Perhaps the most striking of these celestial testimonies to a Divine Mind are the exquisite balancings and proportionings of forces and motions that secure to immense and complex systems of planets and suns perfect stability from age to age; so that not a single well authenticated case of collision between two worlds has ever been noticed. Millions of chances to one against this, without the determination and superintendence of a Divine Providence !

2. *God is one.*—The presence and dominance of designing Mind throughout the astronomical realm being conceded, the inquiry arises whether this designing Mind is singular or plural—whether Nature is the work of one Deity or of several Deities, (possibly of a divine syndicate,) occupying about the same plane of being?

To this important question, which really asks whether monotheism or polytheism should be the religion of the world, Astronomy gives a clear answer—a clearer answer than we can get from the earth alone : for men like the Persians have been perplexed by the presence of good and evil, of pleasure and pain, of the fair and the ugly, of the useful and harmful, of life and death, side by side in this world, and have asked whether Ormusd *and* Ahriman are not the solution of the riddle.

Large material for an answer to this question is given in terrestrial facts. Taking the Bible conception of God with its setting of related doctrines, it can be shown, and has been shown, that the hypothesis of one such God will explain all Nature as we know it at least quite as well as the hypothesis of two or more Deities, and that therefore we are bound by reason and the accepted canons of science to accept the simpler

hypothesis. But this conclusion is greatly emphasized when we extend our view to other worlds.
There is wonderful variety in the celestial regions;
but it is all embedded in a wonderful, all perme-
ating, all embracing unity. So plainly does this
unity manifest itself in the celestial mechanics
that no astronomer is in danger of being a poly-
theist, whatever other dangers he may be in. If
he believes in a God at all, he sees his unity in
every part of the sky. If he worships at all, it is
before a single throne on which sits but one eternal Person, the author and framer of all that eye
or telescope or Calculus discovers.

All the planets and moons proximate spheres,
all of them, as far as we can see, rotating ; all
moving in orbits about the same centre ; all correlated so to one another as to make one stable system ; this system correlated with other systems
into a stable group ; this group correlated with
other groups into a stable cluster ; and so on indefinitely until at last we come to one all-compre-
hending system, with its untold millions of worlds,
full of millions of mighty and intricate movements
which yet are so admirably adjusted and proportioned to one another that steadfast equilibrium is
secured and universal safety and order reign from
age to age—all secured by the presence of a few

simple principles everywhere. Everywhere motion as a mighty factor of equilibrium. Everywhere gravity with its one law. Everywhere the three laws of Kepler in full sight or half ambushed. Everywhere light shooting the same rainbow shafts from its golden quiver. Everywhere space warmed, lighted, and governed by incandescent and locomotive suns. Everywhere system framed into system, as the parts of a house are framed together to make one serviceable whole. Broad lines of sympathy, resemblance, interdependence run everywhere through the heavens, as run the veins and arteries and nerves through animal bodies.

Just as the general resemblance between animals enables Comparative Anatomy to foresee what will be found in the human system, so the great resemblances between the different parts of the astronomical realm have enabled us to forecast many discoveries, long before they were actually made.

Of course there is but one thing to be said. But one thing *is* said to philosophic ears by the voices that fall from the sky. With one consent they proclaim unity of authorship. This unity is the simplest and most natural interpretation of the facts. Such sameness of material, of plan, of process, and of apparent ultimate object (the furnishing of homes for living beings) is just what we would expect from a single author ; and such a single author as the God of the Scriptures is fully equal to the task of making all the heavens, in all their richness and vastness, though these should be found a thousand fold richer and vaster than we yet know them.

3. *God is great.*—After we have been convinced of the Divine existence by immemorial tradition, by our sense of need, by the miraculously attested Revelation, by the enormous superiority of Theism as an hypothesis to account for Nature, it behooves us to get as vivid a conception as possible of the personal greatness of God. We know that his attributes are great, are infinite : but there is a great difference between a cloud as seen in the twilight and the same cloud as painted and illumined by the rising sun. What we need is to have the cloudy vastness which we call omniscience, omnipotence, and eternity, painted and illumined into vividness and realization by full-orbed, effulgent examples of the vast durations, forces, and wisdoms of design and administration which God has established in Nature and by which He has expressed himself. In no science can we find such magnificent examples of these

things as in astronomy. They are to our vague ideas of the natural attributes of God what the light of a great speculum is to the great nebula in Andromeda, only faintly visible to the naked eye.

The Problem of Three Bodies is yet beyond mastery by our most potential science. How much more the Problem of Three Hundred Bodies! That of a system composed of millions of worlds is infinitely beyond even the hope of the most audacious astronomer. And yet a glance at the heavens shows us that God has mastered this despair of our science; for we see there very many such millionaire systems in a state of permanent equilibrium, all the secrets of which God as the inventor and framer must thoroughly understand.

The conditions of stability in our Solar System —a central body much heavier than all its planets and satellites put together; orbits nearly circular, lying in nearly the same plane, and traversed in the same direction—have been ascertained. This achievment is reckoned a splendid triumph of genius and the Calculus. But what human genius is equal to finding the conditions of stability in some enormous globular cluster that has no dominant central orb, and whose orbits cut one another at all possible angles? This is a feat infinitely beyond even the hope of our science. And yet the inventor and framer of such a system, that remains unchanged from generation to generation, must thoroughly know the conditions which he himself has contrived and established.

A single beautiful garden may show a very accomplished gardener : but when we are assured that he has a score or more of similar gardens in different parts of the country, all of which he made and superintends, we conceive a still higher opinion of him as a gardener. A merchant may show much ability in starting and managing a business that covers only a single town and a single branch of trade : but, if we find him successfully extending his operations till they cover the whole nation and almost every commodity, we greatly enlarge our impression of his business faculty. A sovereign may command admiration by his administration of a small principality ; but, if he becomes the head of a great empire and administers a hundred provinces as well as he did his Monaco, we conceive a far greater admiration of his ability as a sovereign than we had before. So, much as we admire and have reason to admire, the vast Mind displayed in the making and furnishing our own world, when we look skyward and find that this world is but an inconsiderable part

17

of the celestial theatre which this Divine Mind
made and administers equally well, we naturally
rise to a grander conception of Him who without
apparent strain extends his earthly sceptre over
all the stars.

To establish and administer so vast and varied
an empire as this argues a breadth and activity
of thought of the most astounding character. Nowhere, outside of Astronomy, do we find signs of
anything like such mighty rushes and battles and
victories of thought and plan and skill as appear
in the glorious systems that wheel their ordered
and enduring pomp through the nightly heavens.
Lo, here is One who is at home in the vastest
affairs, whose congenial element is stupendous
achievement, whose thoughts can go and come from
star to star and from zenith to nadir as easily as our
wings can go from bush to bush! Lo, an executive faculty equal to any emergency or breadth
of application! Lo, endless faculty for detail as
well as for broad superintendence! Lo, powers
so elastic that they never tire, so far reaching that
nothing lies outside of their orbit, so individuali-
zing that the mote in the sunbeam is no more
overlooked than the sun itself! It is a great
throne that looks down upon us from the sky;
but it is not so great as the King who founded
and *fills* it.

The power to produce something out of nothing, by a mere act of will, means a power to annihilate as well as create all things conceivable. Such a power is unspeakably grand. It casts all other powers into the shade. It puts all things within the grasp of its possessor. It is itself condensed omnipotence.

People who believe in God as the framer of Nature, almost or quite without exception, also believe in Him as the Creator of the various elements that compose Nature. When does one get his most impressive conception of creative power? Is it not when he includes in his view, not merely the single grain of sand that he happens to hold in his hand, but that vast host of atoms which compose the shining astronomical realm? Though the power that can produce a single atom out of nothing, by mere willing, is clearly quite as great as that which can smite the deserts of space into Solar systems, yet there is a great difference between the two in power to rouse and impress the imagination. The one conception gives us only the sublime in cause ; the other adds to this the sublime of a vast and glorious effect. We have two sublimities instead of one, just as soon as we lift our eyes from the dust at our feet to the star-dust over our heads.

Then think of the great natural forces revealed in our outlook on the structure and processes of the astronomical earth and heavens. The thunders and lightnings in their might, the winds and waves at their best, the uplift that sets mountains and continents on their high places, the fires that lap up forests and cities in an hour and turn the toughest metals into fluids and vapors, the forces implied in the annual output of vegetable life as well as in tornados, volcanoes, and earthquakes— these are very impressive, but not *so* impressive as the forces implied in the rush of comets and planets, in the fierce disturbances seen in the photo-sphere of the sun, in the sweep of a system of millions of huge worlds at the rate of a million miles an hour, above all in the sum of the dynamics included in the universe system sweeping at about the same inconceivable rate around its centre of gravity. What a POWER must He be who could originate, harness, and keep well in hand such terrible forces! "The thunder of His power who can understand !"—how natural such a thought to a reasonable astronomer as he looks forth from his Uraniberg on the prodigious stellar movements !

The idea of the eternity of God is not an easy one to master : indeed what being, short of God

Himself, has ever compassed it ? But some get a larger and more vivid conception of it than others. Other things being equal, none are likely to get so large and just a conception as those who have striven with the mighty astronomical periods—whose thoughts have climbed as by a ladder from the year of the earth to the year of Neptune, from the year of Neptune to that of our sun, from that of our sun to the hundreds of millions of years that circumscribe the ebb and flow of some stellar perturbations. Wider and wider grows our horizon as we ascend, until at last, from the highest rung of all, we see—never so far, never so far. What are the lives of men, of nations, of dispensations, compared with such a mighty round of æons! The great thought crowds outward the elastic walls of the imagination. The successive flights of conception strengthen our wings. We begin to understand what the Everlasting is like. Its representative is before us. Its spell is upon us. The roar of its boundless ocean is in our ears, and its surf is spraying in our faces. We uncover, we bend low; for are we not at last in the presence of the eternity of God ?

# XVIII.

## Astronomical Religion—II.

HIS VAST EMPIRE.

HIS IMMENSE ACTIVITY.

HIS LOVE OF LAW AND ORDER.

HIS PROVIDENTIAL AND MORAL GOV-
ERNMENT.

NEED OF FULLER REVELATION.

## XVIII.

# ASTRONOMICAL RELIGION—II.

HIS VAST EMPIRE—HIS IMMENSE ACTIVITY—HIS LOVE
OF LAW AND ORDER—HIS PROVIDENTIAL AND
MORAL GOVERNMENT—NEED OF FULLER REVELA-
TION.

The last chapter endeavored to show that the
Modern Astronomy sets in a strong light
the reality, unity, and personal greatness of God.
The present chapter will mention several other
religious facts that are illustrated and emphazised
by the same science—especially in its latest
advances.

1. *God has an amazing empire.*—Until lately the
universe was an exceedingly small thing, as it
appeared in the thought of the most advanced
peoples. To the cultivated Greek and Roman
writers, as well as to the popular mythology of
their times, the whole *cosmos* was hardly more
than the earth : and the earth itself was a small
matter compared with what we now know it to be.
The stars were mere spangles or gaseous tapers.

When better views came, the heavens were still occupied with only about two thousand worlds. When the telescope of Galileo came, the universe became several times larger : and, from that day to this, by successive enlargements of the instrument, the known heavens have gone on expanding until a hundred millions of suns are within view, implying several times that number of planets. Nor is this the end ; though it carries us across a region which light itself could not cross in less than 120,000 years. It is now found that, by adding a camera to the telescope, an additional host of stars is revealed—especially after long exposure of the photographic plate to the same point in the heavens. This plate is more sensitive to faint light than the sharpest eye ; and, unlike the eye, can accumulate faint impressions until they come within reach of sight ; can, as it were, stand on the shoulders of the telescope and command a wider horizon. It is estimated that when the photographic charts of the heavens already agreed upon, and in process in several countries, and by more than twenty telescopes, are completed we shall have within our observation full twenty times the number of stars now shown by our largest telescopes. This will bring the visible stellar host up to two thousand millions.

Is even this the complete total? No astronomer supposes that worlds end where happens to end the vision of our best present instruments. On the contrary, experience assures him that a given increase of space-penetrating power in his instruments is likely to reveal new worlds in as large numbers as ever. One familiar with astronomical history does not find it hard to believe that the unseen heavens are fully as mighty as the seen : he even feels that it would be a safe thing to defy all the researches of the future to reach a district in space where worlds are not. Where is the end? *Is* there any end to the peopled immensities? If one gathers courage and awe enough to pronounce that the stellar universe is co-extensive with infinite space itself, is absolutely without limit in every direction, science has not a single word to say against it, and several words to say for it.

Such is the universe, the *peopled* universe, which God made, over which he reigns, and to every minute particular of which his providence extends. How an ancient theist to whom this earth was the whole creation, or the more recent Tycho to whom this earth was the preponderating centre and metropolis of the sky, would have opened his eyes at such a demonstration as we have of the hugeness of the Divine empire! How trifling, beyond speech, seems the largest earthly kingdom in comparison with this all-embracing monarchy! If there is any awe in a man it will come forth and assert itself on every fresh excursion up and down the tremendous stretches of this celestial empire.

Truly, the King personally so great has a kingdom to match. His sphere is worthy of him. Thought itself grows faint in its presence. What panting Ariel can put a girdle about it? What expert arithmetician can count up its provinces? Behold an empire that never has occasion to dispute over boundaries, for it has none! Behold an empire that fears no attack from without, for to it there is no without. Its horizon sweeps about everything—about everything known and unknown. It is the only empire that has no neighbors. We have heard of the empire on which the sun never sets: here we have one within which all suns rise.

2. *God is a great friend to busy and forceful activity —to an executive way of living.*—The first glance at the heavens seems to discover only absolute rest. But as soon as we begin to look narrowly, and to get beneath the surface of things, we find that everything is in motion after a most wonderful manner. Nothing is at rest. Not an atom but is

moving and working at a tremendous rate. Incessant and mighty activity is found wherever we probe the sky with our eyes or our instruments. Every world, and every particle, seems to have a mission, and to be energetically and remorselessly busy in fulfilling it. Enthusiastic work—from it there is no dispensation and no respite. Day and night, summer and winter, the astronomical forces take no holiday. Some motions are more rapid than others ; the planet, or moon, or sun, has its varying rates of speed ; sometimes, perhaps, a relative rest may be reached for a while in the contest between equal contending forces ; but even in this case the rest is merely relative to a few circumstances. The centre of equilibrium is itself ever on the move. The hub of the chariot wheel, while stationery as to the spokes, is all the while flying over the race course as fast as blooded Arabians can hurry it.

I am not one of those who resolve everything into motion ; yet, beyond doubt, motion is one of the great facts of the physical universe. In astronomy this motion appears in great masses : planets, satellites, and suns rush and wheel so constantly and mightily as to astonish and bewilder us who are so puny, spasmodic, and easily wearied in our action. Tell us of a single object in the sky that stands still. Tell us of a single world that is not traveling faster on its mission than any object that we can impel. From the speed of light to that of Neptune is a large interval; but even Neptune spins along at an average of 12,000 miles an hour. In the heavens, as well as on the earth, activity is the condition of health. Were a world to come to a standstill it would perish. So the whole azure plain above us is throbbing and heaving with vitality. Never was battlefield more alive with advancing, deploying, retreating hosts. No battle ever takes place among the stars; but, seemingly, all the skillful evolutions and scientific moves that precede a great battle are there. No earthly workshop, no mart of trade, no hive of industry, no steaming fleets of commerce or war, are busier at their work than are the shining fleets that go and come in the blue deeps above us. They make no noise about it—at least none that we can hear—but they are vastly executive for all that. Yet there is nothing that seems morbid about this intense activity. Great forces can do great things without straining: and the great careers that are run above us are so within the limits of sanitation that they can be run forever.

Such is the system which God has established and is sustaining in the heavens. Do we not see there an example of what the All-Wise deems the best ordering of things? Have we not pictured there his ideal of how vigorously powers should be exerted, good careers run, and good missions accomplished? Certainly astronomy is not a science that summons to repose—that says to men " Sleep on now and take your rest." It summons to industry, to struggle, to achievement. One feels like going to work, and working vigorously, for very sympathy, as he gazes away at the universal and splendid executiveness that reigns and triumphs throughout the celestial spaces. The swift and ever rushing spheres rebuke his idleness, his languor, his feebleness. In them God has expressed his own forceful nature. In them he has made proclamation that men should do with their might what their hands find to do. It is not the Bible only that tells us that God detests lukewarmness, and loves to see us "zealously affected in a good thing"—the lesson was flaming among the stars long before it was copied into the Book. Both text and copy bid us abhor a vacuum of energy in well-living, as Nature abhors a vacuum of matter.

3. *God is a great friend of law and order.* This is one of the plainest and easiest lessons taught by Astronomy. Whatever else one may deny or doubt, it is not this. The celestial orbs are bound up in such a scheme of interdependent movement as allows their relative situations to be forecast ages ahead. Invisible bonds hold them to their forms, rotations, and revolutions ; to certain times of coming and going ; to definite character and limits of change : even what are called "irregular-ities" and "perturbations" of order are them-selves orderly and creatures of law. · 'The ordinances of heaven stand fast.' Day after day finds the sun running his ancient course. Night after night finds the moon going her his-toric round. Every watchful observatory knows just where to look for any planet ; and, from year to year and from age to age, looks up on the same constellations shining away in the same orderly groupings and imperturbable quiet. Changes there are, slow changes in position and brightness and color, which in the course of ages amount to much ; but they are all the children of law. So the astronomical realm is an object lesson in order. On the earth are many things called *disorders;* many things that defy expectation and computa-tion ; many things, like the weather and individu-

al experiences and historic events, that seem at first view free of all bonds : but in the sky there is at all times the appearance, and as it were the proclamation, of persistent regulation and quiet conformity to irresistible statute that is soothing to the beholder. It is restful to look away from the "accidents" and "uncertainties" and inexplicable tossing of human affairs to the immovable calm and eternal foreordinations that so eloquently speak from their thrones of amethyst and gold.

In our time there is no disposition to question that, at least all physical Nature, is under the dominion of law. Bible believers and unbelievers agree in this : they only differ as to the source and character of these laws. The believer attributes them all to God, and insists that, in addition to the natural forces that originally came from him, should be counted his own personal activity guiding and dominating the whole. The unbeliever excludes this supernatural element from the sum of forces. This is all the difference between the two. And a very great difference it is.

The laws of light, heat, gravity, motion are all capable of definite statement ; are all definitely stated in our text books of science ; and the statements once made are good for all time. These elementary laws, in their combination with one

18

another, give rise to more complex laws which regulate the movements of the heavenly bodies; give
the fixed succession of day and night, the fixed
order of the seasons, the fixed periods of planets
and suns, the fixed though somewhat elastic secular equations that modify within limits the periods
of all the celestial orbs.  As far as we have looked
into the heavens (and that is now a good way)
order *reigns*—order rooting itself in law.  Constancy, subordination, government, harmonious
cooperation—these are the features that, to the instructed gaze, are everywhere pushed to the front ;
often limned as with a sunbeam, sometimes shaded
and faded somewhat, but never disappearing nor
becoming cryptograms.  No astronomer fails to
read them without difficulty in every part of the
sky ; and to most they are about as evident, though
not as alarming, as the characters which a Divine
hand traced before the eyes of Belshazzar.  As far
as our researches have gone, law and order sit on
thrones which only the hand of the Eternal can
overturn ; and we are sure that future researches
will reveal nothing different.

Once men were puzzled by what seemed the
erratic planets.  Their wanderings, apparently,
were guided by no law.  But the law was there,
though it took astronomers some time to find it.

But they found it, unmistakably, at last ; and now, by its means, we can forecast the positions of all the members of our Solar System for ages to come, and at any moment turn our telescope on any one of them. Further, we have come to feel and to know that the astronomic Decalogue which rules in our system is only a specimen of that which rules in every one of the innumerable planetary systems that hide in the remoter heavens.

I do not mean to say that no miracle ever takes place among the astronomies. Law and miracle can co-exist in the same event. You can counteract gravity on the earth, for a little and in particular instances : no doubt God can do the same on a wonderfully grander scale in the sky. He can cast a planet away from the sun as easily as we can cast a pebble into the air. Should he do it, there would be a miracle; for there would be an astonishing effect by a supernatural cause. But there would be no suppression of law, only the dominance of one law over another; that is, the dominance of a supernatural force, working according to its laws, over a natural force working according to its laws. So law and miracle can sit side by side on the same throne and never quarrel.

Surely, if ever there was a friend to law and order, it is he who built and maintains the skies ! They are an object lesson as to what God desires and proposes in the spiritaul realm. As we look at the delicate proportionings and balanced adjustments and orderly ongoings of the systematized firmament, we see a testimony on a magnificent scale that God cannot be tolerant of disorder among any beings, but has given stringent laws to prevent it—laws which he is bent on upholding and to which men will do well to conform.

4. *God credibly maintains over us both a providential and moral government; maintains them in the interest of order and the general welfare.*—It is now universally understood by astronomers that the numberless suns imply as many systems of planets which they light, warm, and control in the interest of intelligent beings like men ; also, that in these vast systems of rational and responsible beings lies the supreme significance and purpose of the visible universe. It exists for their sake. The imposing materialism is for the more imposing and important spiritualism. Houses of all grades, from cabin to palace, are for the sake of inhabitants.

Astronomy shows that God is intelligent and powerful enough to administer an efficient government over these responsible beings (among whom we stand), on both providential and moral lines ; also, that he is disposed to do it. For, we see that he is disposed to regulate, most thoroughly and vigorously, the physical universe according to its nature ; and it follows that he must be still more disposed to regulate, thoroughly and vigorously, according to its nature, that vastly more important universe of intelligent and moral beings for the sake of which the other was made. Of course God has his wishes and purposes in regard to this supreme department of his empire, as well as his measures for securing the fulfilment of these purposes. The only two possible systems of measures are the providential and the moral. He can restrain, impel, and direct us by various appeals to our voluntary and responsible natures, and he can also do it by the pressure of circumstances that do not appeal to the principle of free choice. Whatever his purposes in making us ; whatever the courses he wishes us to take and characters to form, and experiences to have ; it is plain from what we see on the surface of our astronomy that he has both wisdom and power enough to bring to bear on us most potentially both forms of government. On the one hand he can use wind and tide to direct the course of the ship ; and on the other hand he can instruct the captain whom he has put in charge. Of course, God will set himself to bring his fleet of moral beings into the port he has chosen for them by all available means. He will press our wills, and he will press all the rest of us, toward the point he wishes us to gain. That the author of a vast system of moral beings has a purpose in making them, and suitable means for promoting that purpose, and that moral and providential governments are the only possible means, goes without saying with the man who has looked with wide eyes on the boundless intelligence and power and purposefulness displayed in the heavens. In particular, what astronomer will say that the being who framed the orderly and law abiding heavens is not intelligent enough to know and care how men behave, and not powerful and intelligent enough to bring them to account for their conduct, and not purposeful enough to do what he can do, and needs to do, to best promote his object?

To the instructed eye the sky is too full of intelligent purpose, seeking its ends in the use of adapted means and working these means with endless power and skill, to allow us to think that the same thoroughness and efficiency will not be carried into the spiritual realm. Doubtless, the same characteristics which God displays in the one field will appear in the other still more important one. Men do sometimes, on account of their limitations, loosen their girdles and go into vacation as to some of their traits in minor matters; but not even then, unless pushed by their limitations. Except under stress of weather, no ship takes in its sails. God is never under stress. He has no limitations, so far as an astronomer can see.

As to the ends which God has in view in framing and maintaining a moral universe, we are not without some hints of information from astronomical sources. In the heavens God appears to us, not only as a great King, loving law and order and bound to have them at all costs, but as the universal *Father* and *inventor*. Now the instinct and general habit of fatherhood is to seek the welfare of the children. Is not God seeking the welfare of his children? Is he a deplorable exception among fathers? The instinct of the inventor everywhere, so far as we can observe, is to value and cherish his invention. Does not God care for and cherish the great system of intelligent and moral beings which he has invented and impalaced in the astronomical universe?

His dealing with moral beings, however, is not that of inventor and father only. It is also that of a king presiding over vast realms and interests.

No telescope is so feeble as not to disclose this. The one character must be expected to modify to a considerable extent the expression of the other— especially in the case of disloyal subjects. In their case we should be sure of having a government of mingled kindness and severity—sometimes one in which only severity appears ; as often happens under human governments, both parental and civil. There never yet has been a monarch who, however much he loved his people, did not have occasion to do some severe things among them.

There never yet has been a father who could afford to be only a father to his family. So, looking into the heavens where both the father and the king are so abundantly conspicuous, we should say that, in such a world as this, severities and kindnesses would be likely to appear side by side and hand in hand. And it would not be at all surprising if, sometimes, the severity should so dominate and overlay the tenderness as to put it quite out of sight to such eyes as ours, and pass for unmixed hatred and cruelty. Nor at all surprising if, often individual interests should be made to give way to the public welfare. Governments must act for the general good. The man who makes it impossible for the father or king to reconcile kindness to him with kindness to the family or state must expect to suffer, under any righteous administration. People must not lay themselves under the wheels of a chariot that must go on. Alas for Sisera, when the stars in their courses fight against him !

Certainly, the friendship and good offices of a sovereign whose faculties are as mighty as those which appear nightly to every astronomer, must be valuable to the last degree. What great things such a God can do for us, or against us ! There is nothing too great to be hoped from his love— nothing too great to be feared from his wrath. Let the conscious rebel look at the stars and tremble. Let the conscious loyalist look at the stars and rejoice. The man who can unite in his favor both the kingly sceptre and the fatherly heart of God may give the reins to his hopes and triumphant expectations. Surely all things shall work together for his good. He has found the wishing cap of Fortunatus. Son of the Almighty ! all things are yours. The light of morning is behind you, the light of noon is before you; and, even when your face is toward the setting sun, it weaves out of rainbows an aureole for your silvered head.

On the other hand, defiance of God and his government, or even neglect of them, is, in the face of the majestic heavens, preposterous madness :

.19

while, in the face of the majestic heavens, attention, reverence, diligence to glean the Divine will
from all available sources, and obedience to that
will, as far as it can be found or surmised, are
matters of supreme policy and prudence.   The
stars, as well as the Scriptures, say, "There is no
wisdom nor understanding against the Lord."
Certainly, they who have the loftiest conception of
God, who fervently desire the knowledge of his
ways, who are ever feeling after him if haply they
may find him, who are accustomed to invoke the
aid and guidance which he can so abundantly give;
who, in short, put off their shoes from their feet in
the presence of the Infinite—these are the people
most in harmony with the teaching of the stars.
No other method of dealing with God is "the
scientific method", of which we hear so much in
these days.   Whoever takes his cue from modern
astronomy will treat all things pertaining to the
Author of Nature as full of moment to himself
and all men ; and will pay God the compliment of
assuming that he is good till he has been proved
to be bad, of assuming that he is both a benevo-
lent and a righteous being and desires the same
traits in ourselves.

5.  We need, however, in order to best results,
a fuller revelation in regard to some of the fore-

going matters than astronomy furnishes; as well as a revelation of many things concerning which our science gives no hint.

Among the proclamations which the skies make on religious matters is one of their own insufficiency. They speak to us loudly of the power and wisdom of God, and even whisper enough of his character and government to leave us, as the Scriptures say, 'without excuse for not gloryfying him as God.' At the same time, their language as to the love and righteousness of the Almighty, is not as clear and emphatic and easily translated into the world's vernacular as could be wished. A conclusion that lies at the end of a long chain of arguments is apt to be dim. We need to have God affirm it without argument—thus setting it at the focal distance of many near-sighted people. We need such historic examples of his equity and tenderness as the Scriptures supply. We need to see vividly, what every person ought to see, that our relative insignificance in the universe does not involve our being overlooked, or insufficiently attended to, by our Creator; and that even our sinfulness does not set up inseparable barriers between us and the Divine favor. We need a minuter itemizing of the divine will than Nature can supply. We need to know (not guess) whether there is help for sinners ; and, if so, to what extent, and in what way. The heavens reveal no miracles. They utter no prophecies. They contain no historic illustrations of the Divine government. They encourage us with no promises. They are forever silent as to Christ, and the Holy Spirit, and the incarnation, and an expiatory sacrifice, and the resurrection of the dead, and a blessed immortality open to all and forfeitable by all. What they tell us, taken in connection with the law written in our hearts and the religious traditions afloat in every land, is sufficient to bind the conscience to a certain faith in God and to a righteous way of living, but not sufficient to be as mightily impressive and authorative as men need.

In fine, the heavens proclaim the need of further revelation about as loudly as they do the elementary religious facts we have stated. Silence itself has sometimes a loud voice. Whispers in a teacher are better than silence ; but strong, sonorous speech is better still. Chirographs, decipherable with difficulty by specialists, are better than no writing at all; but typewriting so legible that he who runs may read is a much surer instructor and a wonderful saving of time and strength.